LONE STAR VALENTINE

BY
CATHY GILLEN THACKER

D1635725

MILLS & BOON

All rights reserved including the right of reproduction in whole or in part in any form. This edition is published by arrangement with Harlequin Books S.A.

This is a work of fiction. Names, characters, places, locations and incidents are purely fictional and bear no relationship to any real life individuals, living or dead, or to any actual places, business establishments, locations, events or incidents. Any resemblance is entirely coincidental.

This book is sold subject to the condition that it shall not, by way of trade or otherwise, be lent, resold, hired out or otherwise circulated without the prior consent of the publisher in any form of binding or cover other than that in which it is published and without a similar condition including this condition being imposed on the subsequent purchaser.

® and ™ are trademarks owned and used by the trademark owner and/or its licensee. Trademarks marked with ® are registered with the United Kingdom Patent Office and/or the Office for Harmonisation in the Internal Market and in other countries.

Published in Great Britain 2015
by Mills & Boon, an imprint of Harlequin (UK) Limited,
Eton House, 18-24 Paradise Road, Richmond, Surrey, TW9 1SR

© 2015 Cathy Gillen Thacker

ISBN: 978-0-263-25115-9

23-0215

Harlequin (UK) Limited's policy is to use papers that are natural, renewable and recyclable products and made from wood grown in sustainable forests. The logging and manufacturing processes conform to the legal environmental regulations of the country of origin.

Printed and bound in Spain
by CPI, Barcelona

Cathy Gillen Thacker is married and a mother of three. She and her husband spent eighteen years in Texas and now reside in North Carolina. Her mysteries, romantic comedies and heartwarming family stories have made numerous appearances on bestseller lists, but her best reward, she says, is knowing one of her books made someone's day a little brighter. A popular Mills & Boon® author for many years, she loves telling passionate stories with happy endings, and thinks nothing beats a good romance and a hot cup of tea! You can visit Cathy's website, cathygillenthacker.com, for more information on her upcoming and previously published books, recipes and a list of her favorite things.

WAKEFIELD LIBRARIES & INFO. SERVICES	
30000010339893	
Bertrams	10/02/2015
	£3.99

Chapter One

"Rumor has it, you and Lily McCabe have been on the outs with each other for the past eight years."

More like six, Gannon Montgomery corrected silently. Although it *seemed* longer since the two of them had shared a laugh. Or even a smile.

The relaxation he'd felt during the rare morning ride fading fast, he led his horse into the barn. "What's your point?" Gannon demanded.

Rex Carter stepped back. "The last thing Laramie, Texas, needs is a young female mayor."

Gannon could see how the once-popular good old boy opposite him could think that. He pulled off the saddle and removed the bridle, bit and reins. Hung them on the wall outside the stall. "Lily's not that young. Just a few years shy of me."

And, if memory served, incredibly sexy and smart, to boot.

Rex narrowed his gaze. "She's twenty-nine."

Gannon rubbed down the gelding, gave the horse plenty of water, then shut the stall door. He walked over to the sink at the rear of the barn to wash his hands. "Which, as it happens, is old enough for a lot of things. Including running for public office in Laramie County."

Rex slapped his Stetson against the leg of his custom Western suit. "She's an attorney, not a politician."

The more things changed in the rural Texas area he'd grown up in, the more they stayed the same. Gannon sure was glad he now resided in Fort Worth. "Well, tell that to all the people who voted for her," he retorted mildly.

As if recalling he'd been beaten in a landslide by the pretty and personable Lily McCabe, and forced to return to the real estate business his family owned, Rex scowled and ran a hand through his short, graying hair. "The point is, you're not the kind of 'celebrity judge' the committee had in mind for the First Annual Laramie, Texas, Chili Cook-Off and Festival. And Mayor McCabe shouldn't have asked you to do the honors."

Gannon strode out into the unseasonably warm February day. He admired the rugged scenery and let the sage-scented breeze roll over him. "Lily didn't have anything to do with my selection." The request had come from a friend of his mother's, who'd *erroneously* thought dragging Gannon back to join in the festivities would lead him to abandon his high-profile career and return home permanently.

"I agreed to do it because I figured it would be fun."

And maybe give me a chance to mend fences with Lily, at long last. Assuming I could get her to put our old disagreements aside. A pretty big if, given her stubbornness and the acrimoniousness of the words that had been exchanged.

Gannon turned his gaze away from the clear blue skies. "And I thought you were here to talk about the sale of my family's ranch."

Which was—Gannon admitted guiltily, looking at the neglected grounds around the house and barns—in pretty sad shape. Mostly because neither he nor his mother had had the time or inclination to put any work into the defunct cattle ranch since his dad had died five years prior.

Rex straightened, all savvy go-getter once again. "I've definitely developed a plan for the Triple M." He paused to look at Gannon, long and hard. "But to get you and your family top dollar, I'm going to need your full cooperation on every level."

LILY McCABE LISTENED to her assistant, her decision made as soon as the name was uttered. There was no way she wanted this particular Blast From Her Past. Her hand tightened on the telephone receiver that was, like almost everything else in the town hall, many years out of date. "Tell him I'm too busy to see him, but thank him for stopping by."

"Tell him yourself," an achingly familiar male voice suggested from the open portal of her private office.

Lily's gaze lifted, and there he was. Gannon Montgomery. Big as life. Clad not in the elegant suit and tie she would have expected, but in a faded pair of jeans more suitable to his rodeo days, and a navy blue shirt that brought out his midnight eyes. His belt bore a championship buckle, and his brown leather boots were as comfortably worn as the Stetson he held against his thigh.

"Never mind." Lily set down the phone with a sigh.

Ignoring the sensual tilt to his firm masculine lips, she pushed back her chair and stood. Then, remaining behind her large mahogany desk, she propped her hands on her hips. And tried, without success, not to notice how good he still looked. Even with his thick, short dark brown hair all rumpled, and a sandpapery-rough hint of beard rimming his chiseled face. Realizing she'd been staring, Lily dropped her gaze and found herself in even more tantalizing territory. Shoulders broad enough to lean on. Muscular chest and taut abs, all just begging to be touched. Not that she ever would.

Not after everything they'd once said.

And meant…

Lily's eyes shot upward, heat filling her face.

"How did you get past my secretary?" she demanded. Dimples appeared on either side of Gannon's rakish grin. He lifted a big square palm. "Good looks and charm. Same as always."

An unwelcome rush of excitement roaring through her veins, Lily watched Gannon shut the door behind him and stride toward her.

Doing her best to project an aura of professional cool, she

lifted a chastising brow first at him and then at the closed door. "Is that really necessary?"

He dropped his hat on a chair, every bit as confident— and maddeningly chivalrous—as she recalled. "Given what I have to tell you, yes."

What was it about Texas men? she wondered. Always thinking the women in their life needed protecting, whether the women wanted that or not! She blew out a gusty breath and waited, with barely contained impatience, as Gannon roamed the Laramie mayor's office, taking in the photos of her four-year-old son on her desk, the many plaques and awards on the wall. He turned back to her, smelling of fresh air, soap and man. "First off, thanks for selecting me to be on the judges panel for Laramie's First Annual Chili Cook-Off and Festival."

Lily grimaced. "I had nothing to do with it. It was your mother and Miss Mim." The retired town librarian, who had known them all as kids. "She's chairwoman of the event. Although, for the record, we all knew you'd be in town before then, since your mother's newest statue is going to be unveiled in the town square day after tomorrow."

Dark brow furrowing, Gannon paused. "Have you previewed my mom's new artwork?"

She caught the undertone of worry in his low timbre. "No one in town has." She paused. "I'm guessing you haven't, either?"

Gannon shook his head. "My mother is keeping her sculpting studio under lock and key."

Lily knew the retired art teacher had only been selling her work for a few years now, but was looking to make a splash with the work the town had commissioned for the upcoming festival. "Is that usual?"

"No."

Lily told herself not to attach any particular significance to that. "I'm sure it will be amazing."

He nodded tensely.

Deciding letting the situation get too personal could only lead to trouble, Lily pursed her lips. "Back to your invitation to judge…"

Broad shoulders flexed beneath his blue cotton shirt. "You were out of the loop on that," he concluded with humor, not nearly as insulted by her derisive remark as she would've wished him to be. "So noted."

As was much else…

Figuring if he was going to give her the lazy once-over, she may as well do the same to him, Lily let her glance admire the strong masculine planes of his handsome face before dropping once again to the sinewy contours of his chest and flat washboard abs. Lower still, the denim cloaked his long masculine legs and…

With effort, she forced her attention back to his taunting gaze and took a deep breath to allay the slight tremble of her knees. Then, in a slightly strained voice, she admitted, "Although if it had been up to me, counselor…" Given their former rancor and how closely the chili cook-off would force them to work together…

"I would not have been your first choice to be the head judge and the grand marshal of the parade?" he concluded softly.

Lily lifted her chin. "Probably not."

He sauntered nearer, the warmth of his big body radiating outward. "You know, we *could* just call a truce."

Surmising he was about to hit on her, Lily rolled her eyes. "Or not."

He peered at her. "You sure you're a politician?" Hands flat on the paper-strewn surface of her desk, he leaned toward her. "'Cause most politicians I know are prone to copious displays of kissing up."

Or, in this case, just kissing.

Trying not to think about how long she had wanted to do that and somehow managed not to, Lily cleared her throat.

"So you said there was another reason you were here?" she prodded in a crisp, businesslike tone.

For both their sakes, she wanted to get this tête-à-tête over with as soon as possible.

"Right." Gannon pivoted away from her and went back to look at the photo of her and the current Texas governor, taken shortly after she had been sworn in.

He bypassed the hat taking up one of the upholstered chairs in front of her desk, and dropped lazily into the other. Then he stretched his long muscular legs out in front of him. "Rex Carter wants to oust you from your position as mayor."

Lily sent a glance heavenward, cursing all the unnecessary drama. "Tell me something I *don't* know," she replied, deadpan.

"He's serious about proving you unfit for office."

Trying not to think how much she loved Gannon's ruggedly chiseled features, as he stared at her with that look of worry on his handsome face, she sat down behind her desk and folded her hands in front of her. "And I'm serious about proving that I'm more than capable."

A note of disbelief crept into his voice. "You really don't care what Rex's plans are?"

Lily hesitated. She did and she didn't. "I can't govern effectively if I spend all my time worrying about what everyone else is doing."

"Even if the plan is to wreak as much havoc as possible on your weekend-long Valentine's Day fund-raiser?"

"Rex loves Laramie," she replied. "I think when it comes right down to it, he won't want to see the town embarrassed. Especially since his family still has a business here, and could very well stand to profit if the chili cook-off is a success."

Gannon paused. "I think you may be naive about him."

Anger stabbed her heart, quick and brutal.

"And I think," Lily responded just as candidly, rising yet again, "that is something you have said to me before."

YES, GANNON THOUGHT UNHAPPILY, it was something he had said. And Lily had resented it so much she had ended their friendship. Although in that instance, too, he had turned out to be right.

A fact that had made her begrudge his innate protectiveness even more...

As she came around the desk toward him and then moved past him toward the door, he could see not much had changed.

Lily was still as gorgeous as ever, he noted, as he, too, got to his feet. Still liked to wear heels that made the most of her incredible showgirl legs. Her honey-blond waves tumbled just past her shoulders, with a swoop of long sexy bangs across her forehead. Standing half a foot shorter than him, at five foot nine, she was lithe and graceful, curvy in all the right places. A fact illustrated by the trim navy suit skirt and silky white shirt that adorned her delectable body.

"I said that with good reason, as it turned out," Gannon shot back before he could stop himself. Her ex had treated her—and the son she'd eventually had with him—like dirt.

Lily flushed.

"That's a matter of opinion," she reiterated tightly.

The phone on her desk buzzed. Once, then again.

Looking grateful for the interruption, Lily strode back to answer it. "Yes?" She listened, then cast a look at Gannon over her shoulder. Harrumphed loudly. "Did Mr. Montgomery pay you to say that?"

Say *what*? Gannon wondered.

"No, I guess not," Lily continued, miserably. She rubbed her temples. "And there are *how many* of them?"

Then she muttered something beneath her breath he couldn't quite catch but sensed was very unladylike. "No. For heaven's sake, don't have them wait in the lobby! Show them to the conference room down the hall from my office. Yes. *Including him.* Tell them I'll be right in. Yes. Yes!"

Lily hung up the phone.

Her hand was shaking.

Her face pale.

Then red.

Then pale again.

Seeing her so distressed, it was all Gannon could do not to wrap his arms around her and make everything okay. "Rex Carter?" he guessed.

Lily scoffed and ran a hand through her bangs, pushing them off her forehead. "Worse," she moaned. "My son's father."

"Bode Daniels." The star quarterback for the Dallas Gladiators football team.

Lily's shoulders sagged as she nodded miserably. "And his sports agent, PR rep, publicist and two lawyers."

That was quite an entourage. Gannon studied the expression on her face. "And you had no idea they were coming?"

"None." Lily paled again as outside in the corridor a collection of convivial voices rose and fell. Their footsteps faded.

"Do you need a lawyer?" Gannon asked, only half joking.

"I already have one. Liz Cartwright-Anderson."

Who was, Gannon reflected, also a mutual friend.

Lily reached for her suit jacket and slipped it on. "But Liz is on vacation with her family right now, at Padre Island." And she was the best Laramie County had to offer.

Desperation mingled with the worry in her long-lashed turquoise eyes.

It got to him—big-time.

With effort, he once again resisted the impulse to take her in his arms and smooth a hand through her hair. Anything to comfort her. "Want me to fill in for her? I'm a family-law attorney, too."

Lily looked tempted for a nanosecond, but then she shook her head. "No. I've got it." She paused, as if steeling herself emotionally for the battle ahead. "I trust you can see yourself out…?"

Gannon sighed. She'd made it clear a long time ago that

she didn't want—or need—him. Probably never would. "Sure," he said, just as coolly. "And, Lily?"

Their eyes held. For a moment, something shimmered between them, lingered like a dust mote on the air, then disappeared altogether. "Good luck with that—whatever it is." He jerked his head in the direction the voices had gone.

She nodded. Her expression turbulent, she took off toward her meeting.

Gannon made it as far as the lobby in the town hall before the second thoughts set in. None of this was his problem. Lily'd articulated that numerous times. And yet…she was in trouble. And maybe her son, too. He could feel it in his gut.

He'd been brought up to never ever leave a lady in distress. That went double when an innocent little kid was involved.

He wasn't about to start now.

Chapter Two

"I just need you to modify the custody arrangements," Bode Daniels claimed.

This was news. Feeling as if she'd just sustained a punch to the gut, Lily sat down opposite him at the conference table. Both surrounded and outnumbered by her ex and his entourage, she worked to contain her shock and dismay. "In what way?" she asked calmly.

Bode rocked back in his chair and smiled charismatically, while his team of professionals wordlessly urged him on. "Give me custody of Lucas for a while."

As if it were just that simple, Lily thought in astonishment. *Who the heck does this guy think he's dealing with?* Emboldened by the fact that she had long ago ceased being a woman who could be easily charmed or seduced, she returned, just as easily, *"Why?"*

Sensing resistance, Bode tucked his hands into his armpits and set his jaw. "It's complicated."

Lily looked right at him. As her confusion faded, anger took its place. Another beat of silence fell. "I've got time."

Her ex shoved a hand through his cropped white-blond hair, then adopted the earnest-but-likable look he had perfected for his signature cologne ads and continued, "You know I didn't exactly have the best season last year."

"No kidding," Gannon Montgomery agreed cheerfully as he walked in unannounced, tray of vending machine coffees in one hand, a flat of pastries he'd commandeered from the break room in the other.

Lily turned toward him, relieved for the interruption.

As if reading her mind, Gannon winked.

"Exactly *who* are you?" Bode's sports agent asked, clearly as surprised to see Gannon there as Lily was.

Bode dismissed Gannon with a glare. "He's one of Lily's law school buddies."

Or at least Gannon had been, Lily noted silently, until Bode had come into the picture, just as she was getting ready to graduate.

"Actually," the senior lawyer on Bode's team, a distinguished man in his late forties, corrected, "this is Gannon Montgomery—one of the top family-law attorneys in Fort Worth."

The other attorney, a young, good-looking woman with wiry ebony hair, squinted at Gannon. "Are you representing Ms. McCabe?" She clearly seemed to hope not.

Gannon looked at Lily.

He'd crashed her meeting and successfully intercepted Bode's ridiculous demands. Now the ball was in her court.

Figuring it wouldn't hurt to have another member on her legal team, particularly if it temporarily set her opponents off their game, Lily said what she knew to be the truth—at least in several other cases. "Mr. Montgomery is 'of counsel' with my family-law attorney, Liz Cartwright-Anderson."

Meaning Gannon could advise on legal matters but wouldn't do anything unless it became necessary, and then only at her current attorney's discretion.

Which, Lily firmly intended, would not be the case.

Gannon beamed. As always, glad to be of service, even if it was only because he had strong-armed his way into the situation.

Lily stifled a small sigh.

"So where were we?" Gannon asked pleasantly, pulling up a chair and taking his place next to Lily.

"Bode wants me to hand over custody of Lucas for a little while."

"Ah." Gannon nodded, then turned to Bode, saying drolly, "Going to play the sympathy card with the press and public?"

His legendary cool fading, Bode's eyes started to glaze over with barely contained anger, and Lily could see the skin on his neck reddening.

A telltale sign that he was about to implode.

But before Bode could do or say anything untoward—like leap across the table and grab Gannon by the collar—his attorney interjected sternly, "Bode is Lucas's father. And up to now, my client's had precious little time with his offspring."

"And whose fault is that?" Lily spit out, before she could stop herself.

Gannon reached over and put a staying palm on her wrist. His touch sent an unexpected jolt of warmth rippling through her, which left her feeling even more flustered.

As it was meant to, his touch infused her with a sudden burst of calm.

"Bode will be a free agent in another month," the sports agent continued.

So what? Lily thought impatiently but said instead, "Which means he could go to another team."

"In another far-flung part of the country," his agent emphasized. He paused to let his words sink in. "Bode doesn't want that."

Nor, if she were honest, did Lily. It was hard enough to arrange Lucas's once-a-year meet and greet with his dad now.

The agent continued, "Right now, the Dallas Gladiators are hesitating to offer an early extension of his current contract to Bode. They are concerned he is not as popular with their fans as he once was."

The public relations guru who managed Bode's "brand" jumped in. "Our research has shown a big part of that is because Bode never fully recovered from the fallout over—"

"Dumping Lily after their whirlwind romance, publicly

discounting his part in Lily's pregnancy and then marrying a Venezuelan supermodel and promptly fathering two more children with his new bride—all the while ignoring his son with Lily?" Gannon set the record straight with a taunting smile. "Until the results of a court-ordered paternity test made that impossible, that is. Then, of course, Mr. Daniels had no choice but to own up."

The PR expert must have noticed the way Bode was bristling, because she suddenly put her hand on the superstar athlete's wrist. "Unfortunately for all, I think the confusion regarding Lucas's paternity is what most people remember," she said with a brand manager's aplomb. "Which is why, for everyone's sake, we need to remedy that perception, and make sure everyone knows what a devoted daddy Bode is to *all* his children. That starts with modifying the custody agreements."

Figuring this charade had gone far enough, Lily stood. "Actually, I like things just the way they are." She smiled tightly.

Gannon gave her an "atta girl" look.

Then, without further ado, Lily walked to the door and opened it wide. "Now, if you all will excuse me," she stated unequivocally, "I really have to get on with my day."

GANNON HUNG AROUND long enough to make sure everyone vacated the conference room.

"Talk sense into her," one of the lawyers said, handing Gannon his card.

"It'd be best for everyone," the female attorney agreed.

With a muted look of frustration, Bode strode off. His entourage hurried to catch up with him as he exited Laramie Town Hall. Gannon took the platter of pastries back to the break room, commandeered two from the plate and returned to Lily's office.

The door was shut.

He knocked and, without waiting for an answer, headed in.

Lily was sitting at her desk, suit jacket off, her head in her hands. She looked up, the weight of the world in her eyes. "Really?"

Given the fact there were any number of things she could call him to task on, he countered with an innocuous smile and a lift of one confection-filled hand. "Pastry?"

Her spine stiffened. "No."

He tore his gaze from the way her breasts were pressing against the soft fabric of her blouse and concentrated instead on the flush of angry color sweeping her delicate cheeks.

Knowing he had never wanted to take her into his arms more than he did at that very moment, he tilted his head. "Something to drink, then? Lukewarm coffee? Bottle of scotch…?"

She stifled an unwilling smile. "You are a laugh a minute, counselor."

Purposefully, he shut the door behind him, enclosing them in her private space. "I try."

Her chin lifted another notch. "And you shouldn't have barged in to the conference room."

He ambled toward her. Set an apple Danish on her desk, just in case, then waited until she rocked back in her chair and met his eyes. "I'm aware you don't need protecting," he said.

She released another long, quavering breath. "Then why did you come to my rescue?"

She had a point. He wasn't normally inclined to insert himself into situations where he clearly did not belong.

"Don't know." He inhaled the familiar scent of her signature freesia perfume, let his glance drift over the sexy waves of her honey-blond hair. "Habit?"

Lily groaned and put her face back in her hands.

Dropping down into a chair, he took a bite of the pastry. It had been sitting out for a while and was, as a result, rather stale. But still delicious in its own way.

Remembering how Lily always tended to reach for the sweets when stressed, he asked, "Want to talk about it?"

She pinched off a bite of pastry, held it between her fingers, then let it fall. Her gaze still on the bite she couldn't bring herself to eat, she shook her head, admitting in a low, strangled tone, "There are no words."

Gannon couldn't fault her for being despondent. That didn't mean he wouldn't try to goad her back into fighting mode, however.

"For what kind of jerk your ex is? 'Cause if you need help—" he waggled his brow "—I can think of a few very fitting adjectives."

She smiled, despite herself. Tore off another bite of pastry. Thought about eating it, then set it down again, without tasting. "He wasn't always like that," she said sadly.

He had made his own mistakes in the romance department, too. Gannon gave a sympathetic nod. "I know that."

When Lily had first met Bode Daniels, the athlete had been ambitious to a fault but not a complete jackass. Just not the right guy for a softhearted woman like Lily. "I liked your ex better when he was the backup quarterback for the Gladiators, instead of a star player, too." Something about sitting on a bench during most of the games humbled a guy. Million-dollar contracts, limitless endorsement deals and star QB status did the opposite.

Anxiety crept into her pretty turquoise eyes.

Gently, Gannon asked, "Do you think he's serious about gaining custody of Lucas?"

Lily stiffened her spine. "No," she said, oblivious to the way her action had also lifted the luscious swell of her breasts.

Ignoring the pressure building at the front of his jeans, he encouraged her to continue.

"The only thing Bode really cares about is playing football." She paused, thinking, and raked her teeth across her lower lip. "In fact, I'm sure this wasn't even his idea. He just got dragged into it by the members of his dream team, because it's time for a new contract." She sighed, shook off the veil of tension and predicted sagely, "This will all be over in a month, or less, as soon as he inks a new deal with the Gladiators."

Given what was at stake, Gannon was not as sure it would be over. Or even if a new contract would be offered, given Bode's lackluster performance the previous season. There was one thing he did know, though. Star athletes who were faced with dwindling careers could be as tough as nails to deal with.

Gannon downed the rest of his pastry. Finished, he wiped his hands on the napkin and forced himself to think like a lawyer, rather than Lily's former friend and current—if only by default—protector. "What is your existing arrangement?" he asked casually.

Lily pushed away from her desk. "I have full physical custody, so Lucas resides with me." She stood and paced to the window overlooking the town square. "Bode has the option to see Lucas every other weekend and one night during the week."

Or, in other words, the status quo for a noncustodial parent, Gannon thought. Unable to bear the discouragement in her low tone, he rose and went to join her. "Has Bode taken advantage of that?"

Lily swung toward him, shivering slightly, her soft lips slanting downward. "Once a year—usually in the preseason—Bode asks me to take Lucas to a park in Dallas so Bode can be photographed with Lucas on the playground. Those 'spontaneous' photos of father and son are then released to the tabloid and legitimate press." Cupping her hands beneath her elbows, she concluded bitterly, "Because Bode is so rarely seen with Lucas, his personal PR team makes sure that they get a lot of play in the media."

Gannon could recall seeing a few of them himself. They'd done the trick, all right; even he had imagined Bode and Lucas had a great father-son relationship. "What about Christmas?"

A shadow crossed Lily's lovely face. "Bode spends what time off he has in Aspen, with Viviana and their two babies, and an assortment of nannies and other help."

Gannon couldn't say he was surprised. "Has Bode ever asked to take Lucas with him on vacation or any other holiday?"

Lily sent him a droll look that upped his pulse another notch and made him want to console her even more. "What do *you* think?"

"He has not."

"Correct." She shifted her weight from one leg to the other, calves tautening sexily, her hips swaying beneath the snug fabric of her skirt. "Although according to the terms of our custody agreement, Bode is entitled to have his son with him on alternate holidays."

Gannon's eyes shifted upward, and his blood flowed hotter in his veins. He lifted his gaze from the tempting roundness of her derriere, guessing, "Bode just doesn't take advantage of it."

"It's not what Viviana would want. Me, either, actually," she continued with grim determination. "Considering how Viviana feels about the fact that Bode had a child with someone else before her."

A silence fell.

Lily drew a breath. Then she raked her fingers through her hair, pushing the fringe of bangs off her face. "I'm sure this will all blow over. There are other ways for Bode to look good in the press in the next few weeks. I'm sure he and his team will find them."

Gannon studied her outward control, which seemed fragile at best. "So you don't want to counter with the offer of a couple of well-timed photo ops in the meantime, just to ward off any more trouble?"

Lily paused, then shook her head. "I let Bode be photographed with Lucas every summer because I want him to have some contact with his dad," she explained. "And realistically, to date, I knew that was the only way it was ever going to happen."

If—and only if—there was something Bode could get out of it for himself, Gannon thought.

Chin set, she continued, "I'm not going to let my son be used as a pawn in his father's contract negotiations. Because I'll tell you what would happen, Gannon. My ex would be all in, until the moment the new contract was signed. Then he'd want Lucas out of the way, again."

She returned to her desk and picked up a framed photo of her little boy, looking down at it fondly. Smoothing her fingertips across the glass, she said, "Up until now, Lucas has been too little to really understand what was going on."

Gannon hadn't had the pleasure of meeting Lucas yet. Maybe soon?

Walking over to take a look at the photograph, too, Gannon did some quick calculations. "He's what? Four now?" With the same wavy blond hair, turquoise blue eyes and piquant features of his mother. The same lithe, fit frame, the same intelligent welcoming regard…

"Yes." Lily swallowed hard. "And I'm not going to tell my son that we're suddenly changing all the arrangements and he's going to live with his dad part of the time only to have to turn around a month later and tell him that he's not. And then have him confused and upset, for no reason."

Put that way… "I wouldn't allow it, either," Gannon said.

Lily paced away from her desk, took a deep breath and set her hands on her hips. She gave Gannon a look that said while she was glad they were in agreement, she was no more willing to let him close to her again now than she had been the last time they'd seen each other years ago.

They'd argued heatedly back then…and clearly she was in no mood to forgive and forget.

She drew a bolstering breath. "I really do have to get back to work."

Getting the message that was his cue to leave, Gannon

retrieved his hat. But he kept his gaze locked with hers. "If you need me—"

"I won't."

He withdrew a business card from his wallet, borrowed a pen from her desk and wrote on the back. Fingers touching hers, he pressed it into her hand. "That's my personal number. I'm available 24/7 until Liz gets back in town." And maybe thereafter, too, if the two of them ever got their friendship back on track.

"I won't need you," Lily repeated, stubborn as ever.

Gannon sincerely hoped that was indeed the case.

"COMPANY, MOMMA!" LUCAS shouted when the doorbell rang, several hours later. "My cousins and the ants are here!"

"Aunts," Lily corrected. Grinning, she followed her son into the foyer.

"That's what I said," Lucas insisted importantly, standing legs braced apart, hands on his hips. "Ant Rose and Ant Violet."

With a grin and a shake of her head, Lily opened the door and ushered their company inside. Unlike the twins in the family—Maggie and Callie—who were identical, Lily and her two closest sisters were fraternal triplets, and hence nothing alike.

Whereas she was tall and blond, Rose was of medium height, with light ash-brown hair. Violet was tall, too, but had very dark brown hair, like their dad's side of the family.

"And Ant Rose brought her baby triplets, too!" Lucas continued as his cousins—two girls and a boy—toddled in with both aunts.

Chaos erupted as greetings were exchanged all around.

When Lucas had finally hugged everyone, he gestured to the play area in the family room adjacent to the kitchen and breakfast nook. "I'm building a barn!" he declared. "And a ranch. And a fence where I can put my cows and horses."

"Let's go see." Violet herded all her nieces and nephews

into the family room. Together, they admired what Lucas had done with his vast trove of wooden architecture-style building blocks and toy farm animals.

Meanwhile Rose—a produce wholesaler and proponent of the Buy Local movement—carried the box of veggies she'd brought for their weekly get-together into the kitchen. "So what's up?" she asked with concern.

"With what?" Lily asked.

"Come on, sis. Don't play dumb." Rose set a dark green head of crisp romaine lettuce, juicy heirloom tomatoes, cucumbers, carrots and radishes on the table. "I heard Bode was in town, along with an entourage. In a stretch limo, no less."

"Oh…that." While she rinsed the lettuce and put it in the salad spinner, Lily explained what had happened.

Rose's expression turned to one of disgust. Having suffered her own quick and ugly divorce, she was not sympathetic to irresponsible, uncaring men. "That man's ego knows no bounds," she said, upset. "Hasn't Bode thought at all about what this would do to his son?"

"Obviously not," Lily murmured. Not that this was a surprise. Her ex never had cared about Lucas—and probably never really would, either, as sad as that was. All that mattered was raising Bode's popularity with the fans in time for a new contract.

"No peeking, Aunt Violet!" Lucas shouted from the other room, while his younger cousins settled down to watch. "I'll call you when I'm done!"

"I'll be waiting," Violet promised. She joined her sisters at the kitchen island. "What's going on?"

Briefly, Rose brought her up to date.

Violet hugged Lily in commiseration. "Too bad you didn't know your ex was coming with his entourage," she said quietly. "You could have had your lawyer there, too."

"Oh, I had one," Lily admitted with mixed feelings. "Although he was uninvited."

Rose's and Violet's brows rose in wordless inquiry.

"Gannon Montgomery was in my office when Bode and the others arrived," Lily explained, doing her best to curtail her emotions. "I sent him on his way, but he crashed the meeting in the conference room anyway."

Another wide-eyed reaction. "And?" her sisters prodded, in unison.

Lily went back to quartering tomatoes. She arranged them around the rim of the salad bowl. "Gannon didn't say much. But clearly his presence put the other attorneys off their game. I think they expected to roll right over me."

"No surprise there," Rose said heatedly. She stepped in to peel and slice the carrots. "Given the way Bode dissed you in the press at the end... If I had been you, I would have thrown him to the wolves from the get-go."

"Instead," Violet recollected, grabbing a cutting board and knife, too, "you made everything a lot easier on Bode than he deserved."

Lily got the makings for a balsamic vinaigrette out of the cupboard, along with a bowl and whisk. "I got what I wanted out of the deal." She dropped her voice to a whisper. "The truth about Lucas's parentage corroborated, full custody and the right to make all the decisions about his care and upbringing on my own."

Rose checked to make sure all four children were still safely out of earshot, then returned to the kitchen island. "What did Lucas think when he saw his dad was in town?" she asked.

Lily whisked the salad dressing together with more than necessary force. "He doesn't know."

Again, her sisters exchanged looks. "You didn't let Bode see him?" Violet inquired in surprise.

Lily looked at her resident-physician sister. "He never asked. He came in with his team of experts for backup, then left when he didn't get what he wanted."

"So what next?" Rose asked as she began setting the table.

Lily shrugged, refusing to borrow trouble. "Nothing that concerns me. Or Lucas."

Violet paused. "You don't think Bode will pursue this?"

When there were other, much easier ways to improve his public image? Lily shook her head. "Nope." Instead, she expected to see Bode visiting sick kids in the children's hospitals, working with the underprivileged or creating a foundation in his name. All with a photographer present.

"What about Gannon Montgomery?" Rose teased, taking a lighter tact. "Are you going to pursue him?"

Flushing guiltily despite herself, Lily took the lasagna from the oven and set it on the stove to cool. "Definitely not!"

Evidently more curious about the lack of love in Lily's life than her own, Violet asked, "Is he going to pursue you?"

Trying not to think about how much the deeply romantic part of her still wanted that to happen, Lily inched off her oven mitts. "Gannon and I put that notion to bed a long time ago." She pushed the image of his handsome face out of her mind. As well as the one of him naked between the sheets that followed. "We found out the hard way that we're too different to even be friends." Never mind lovers!

Rose frowned. "He's still not inclined to compromise?"

"In his case," Lily replied stubbornly, "I'm not, either." Not when she knew how deep the attraction between them still was.

Gannon had devastated her once.

She wasn't going to let him do it again.

To LILY'S RELIEF, there was no further communication from Bode or any member of his team either that evening or the following day.

So it was with a much lighter heart that she went to the unveiling ceremony for the statue by Harriett Montgomery on Friday morning.

The artwork was already on the cement platform that had been built just for it on the town square. Nearly six feet tall, the statue was draped with heavy canvas cloth, secured by ropes.

Around that, a velvet rope line had been set up, giving the statue approximately twenty feet in all directions. A crowd of townspeople, including local resident and Texas patron of the arts Emmett Briscoe, had gathered around the podium erected for the dedication. A videographer had set up as well, to record the ceremony for posterity.

As suspected, Gannon Montgomery was there, too, escorting his mother. Fortunately, he was busy talking to some people he hadn't seen in a while as Lily went over to greet the artist.

Clad in her usually brightly colored attire—today's pantsuit was a vibrant orange—her salt-and-pepper hair drawn back in a tight chignon that emphasized the stark natural beauty of her features, Harriet Montgomery looked both excited and much younger than her sixty-five years.

Lily gave her former high school art teacher a hug hello. "Ready for your big moment?" she asked.

Harriett nodded. "As I explained to you before, I'm going to do the undraping myself. I'd like photos for the paper taken then, and again after I add the final touch."

Lily nodded, not sure what the final touch would be. "The photographer from the Laramie newspaper is all set."

Given that everyone else was there, too, Lily stepped to the podium. She gave a brief introduction to Harriett Montgomery, and then it was time.

Harriett moved past the rope lines. Then pulled off the draping, revealing a six foot high chili pepper on the vine.

It was, as Lily had expected, quite beautiful in a stark, elemental way. And the perfect complement to the Laramie Chili Cook-Off & Festival they were inaugurating, that they hoped would put the town of Laramie, Texas, on the way to fame forevermore.

Still smiling while everyone clapped politely, Harriett posed for the photos she had requested. Then, with the vid-

eographer still filming, Harriett stepped behind the statue
and reached down to do something near the bottom—Lily
wasn't sure what—before straightening again and coming
proudly back to the podium.

Lily looked at the artist in confusion.

Harriett took the microphone and advised the crowd happily, "Wait for it… Wait for it…"

A second later, a faint charcoal-like smell filled the air.

Lily furrowed her brow in confusion.

Then a wispy gray curl of what certainly *looked* like
smoke appeared at the top of the chili pepper stem. Lily
blinked and blinked again.

"Is that…?" Lily turned to Gannon's mother. Out of the
corner of her eye, she noted that Gannon seemed as concerned as she suddenly was.

"Keep waiting," Harriett advised, even more calmly, to
the crowd.

So everyone did.

And then, a second later, flames burst out of the six-foot-
tall chili pepper. And this time there was absolutely no mistake, Lily noted.

The *entire statue* was on fire.

Chapter Three

The fire department had barely put the flames out when former Laramie mayor Rex Carter stepped up to the dais and took the microphone. "This," Rex said, with a derisive good old boy snort, "is what you get when you put a woman in a man's job."

Several people booed him.

Others listened with seeming agreement while the firefighters stood by, watching the red-hot tower continue to spit embers skyward.

Harriett elbowed Rex aside. "Don't blame Mayor McCabe," the artist stated as she stepped up to the microphone. "Lily had no idea what I planned to do. Nor did anyone else."

While the videographer filmed, the Laramie newspaper reporter called out, "Mrs. Montgomery! Why did you light the statue on fire?"

Harriett smiled and explained, "I wanted to complete the work. It's a fire statue—half sculpture and half performance art."

Lily sighed. She wished like heck she had seen this coming. "Well, I wish you would have told someone what you planned ahead of time," she said, not bothering to hide her exasperation.

A number of spectators nodded in agreement.

Harriett Montgomery shrugged, unaffected by all the

negative attention. "I didn't think you'd let me do it if I did. Local statutes and all."

Harriett was right about that, Lily thought in consternation. Both the fire and sheriff's departments had been called to the scene as soon as the flames shot skyward, and the senior officials from both looked mighty unhappy.

Gannon stepped in. He laid a cautioning palm on his mother's shoulder. "I don't think you should say anything more, Mom."

The lawyer in her surfacing, Lily agreed. There was enough reckless behavior here as it was without adding to the liability. "In any case, it's been quite an event," she declared with a tight officious smile.

Rex Carter took another long look at the charred ceramic statue. "You haven't heard the last of this," he muttered to Lily before he strode away.

Realizing she had just given her prior political opponent ammunition against her, Lily watched as the crowd dispersed. Then, hoping to smooth the waters somehow, she went to see how the official investigation was going. Fire Chief Tom Evans scowled at her as she approached. "She's lucky she didn't start a grass fire."

She should have asked a few more questions instead of giving the artist carte blanche when the town had commissioned the work for the chili festival. Lily rubbed her temples to relieve her growing tension headache. "I know."

"I'm tempted to press charges, too," Sheriff Ben Shepherd continued.

Lily lifted a hand. "Please, don't. I'll see it never happens again."

The sheriff scowled. "She will get a warning citation."

"And a bill from our department for the emergency services," the fire chief added.

Lily nodded. "That's fine." Probably a good idea, too. Since, thus far, Harriett Montgomery still didn't seem to recognize she had done anything wrong.

No sooner had the sheriff and the fire chief walked away than Sheriff's Deputy Rio Vasquez came toward her, clipboard in hand. Now what?

"Lily McCabe?" Rio said, although he knew darn well who she was. He handed her an envelope. "You've been served."

AN HOUR LATER, Lily finally had her family-law attorney, Liz Cartwright-Anderson, on the phone. From her office window in the town hall, Lily could see the commotion surrounding the burned-out statue, where resident after resident was walking up to the cordoned-off area to see the remains of the sculpture. "I'm sorry to disrupt your vacation." She went on to explain the nature of the emergency.

"It's okay," Liz said, as cordial and professional as ever. "Given the fact that you only have twenty days to respond to Bode's request for a change in the custody agreement, you're right—we do need to act fast. And what I advise, since I won't be back in the office until Monday or able to do anything until then, is that I hire Gannon Montgomery to temporarily assist me in representing you."

Great—just what I wanted to hear, Lily thought in dismay. But she bit her tongue and let her lawyer continue.

"He's not only helped me out on difficult cases before, but he's also part of the Dallas and Tarrant County bars. He knows the judges and handles a lot of the high-profile custody and divorce cases there. And he's in town, to assist his mother, for the next week or so."

Lily pushed the image of the sexy attorney from her mind. This would be a business request. That was all. "You think he'll do it?"

"Given how much he likes rescuing damsels in distress?" her attorney scoffed. "Of course he will."

Lily knew Liz was right.

Not only did she need Gannon—temporarily anyway—he would probably jump at the chance to help her…or any other woman…in dire straits. It didn't make it any easier to turn to Gannon for help in Liz's absence, of course. But what choice did she have when her son's welfare was at stake?

"What I suggest is that the two of you meet at my office," Liz continued crisply. "Can you do it over lunch?"

Lily had already canceled her lunch date, as well as everything else on her calendar that didn't absolutely have to be addressed that day. "Yes."

"In the meantime, I'll call Gannon and have my paralegal pull all the records so he can start getting up to speed," Liz promised, professional as ever.

BY THE TIME Lily got there at noon, Gannon was already set up in the conference room. As she drank him in from head to toe, Lily imagined he wore an elegant business suit and tie, appropriate for a powerful attorney in Fort Worth.

But back here in the west Texas county where he'd grown up, adorned in jeans, boots and a casual wool sport coat, he was all hard-muscled, take-charge cowboy.

And though she'd never say it to his face, she very much preferred *this* persona.

Of course, right now, when he looked distractedly over her, surrounded by all those legal documents, she knew better than to be fooled by his rugged appearance. He was still very much in full-throttle *attorney* mode.

Figuring he wouldn't have had time to eat, either, she set a Ye Olde Sandwich Shop bag on the table. "Thanks for jumping in to help."

He inclined his head to one side. "Thanks for doing your best to keep my mother out of trouble today."

Still feeling frazzled and on edge, Lily admitted, "It was some morning."

He nodded in mute agreement, his own eyes somber.

Lily gave him his choice of turkey and provolone or ham and cheese. He took the latter. Then she pulled out two bottles of sparkling water, two bags of chips and several napkins.

She had zero appetite but also knew she had to eat. "So what do you think?" she asked, inclining her head at the thick file.

"Looks like Bode's attorneys buried you in motions when this all started."

Lily nodded. The fact she was a lawyer, too, had helped her understand a lot of what was going on—then and now. But she had never practiced family law or become an expert in child custody, and that hurt her ability to deal with any of this strictly on her own.

The empathy in his expression encouraged her to go on.

"His legal team wanted me to just go away. But with Bode assassinating my character in the press and publicly questioning my integrity, I had to do something to protect my reputation."

Especially since Bode and his legal team had been making veiled threats behind the scenes to not only countersue her in civil court for any and all damages done to Bode's reputation, but to bring her up on ethics charges before the State Bar of Texas for knowingly bringing a false paternity suit.

They couldn't have won; they'd all known that. But they could have done untold damage to her career anyway. Luckily, Bode had come to his senses, called his attorneys off at the last minute and consented to the court-ordered paternity test he'd claimed would free him.

Only it hadn't. At that point, once the indisputable facts were brought to light, it had become all about damage control. And money, of course.

Not that Lily had asked for one red cent from him…

Gannon's gaze roved over her features. He regarded her for a long careful moment. "And if you hadn't had so much at stake professionally back then?"

Lily shrugged, not bothering to hide the humiliation and pain she had suffered. "I probably still would have fought him—reluctantly. Not for child support, but for the truth, for Lucas's sake. Better Lucas know from the get-go who his parents are." Than always wonder and have his mother called a liar.

"Even if one of them doesn't seem to want him very much," Gannon remarked, sitting back in his chair.

Lily tore her eyes from the hard sinew of his chest beneath the starched cotton of his shirt. It had been years since the two of them had been friends, never mind meant anything at all to each other, and yet he still amped her pulse. It was so unfair. For so many reasons, he'd been off-limits then. Still was now.

She sighed, doing her best to focus on the situation at hand instead of the ruggedly handsome man opposite her. "So you think taking me to court is a pressure tactic on their part?"

Gannon gave her a barely perceptible nod, ripped open his chips and unwrapped his sandwich. "They want you to know they're going to play hardball unless you immediately give them everything they want."

She studied the disheveled strands of Gannon's dark brown hair. The cool appraisal in his midnight-blue eyes. "You don't think I should," she observed.

"I don't compromise in situations like this," he told her. "I go full throttle, and I advise my clients to do the same." He took a bite of sandwich. She forced herself to eat a little, too.

Her glance fell to the court summons she'd faxed over earlier. "Did you have a chance to read the petition?"

Another nod and grim narrowing of his eyes.

Lily pushed her mostly untouched lunch to the side. Stated unhappily, "He's alleging that I have prevented him from seeing Lucas more than once a year for the past fifty-two months." She knotted her hands into fists and leaned toward him, her fury mounting. "It's not true. All Bode had to do was ask and I would have allowed it." Lily swallowed around the lump in her throat. "He didn't ask."

Gannon paused to make a note.

"The petition also alleges that I refused to let Bode take

Lucas on his annual vacation two days ago. But he never asked for that, either!"

Gannon tilted his head to one side, looking matter-of-fact enough for the both of them. "I expect his team to point out that's only because you threw them all out before they had a chance to get down to the specifics of the request that day."

Lily gasped in indignation and leaped to her feet. "Bode only came here because he wanted half custody of our son to help improve his public persona!"

Gannon grimaced. "That may be how you viewed it, Lily." He paused to let his words sink in. When she would have moved away, he reached across the table and caught her hand in his. His warm touch engulfing her, he continued pragmatically, "*Their* take is that they were just trying to get you to understand how difficult the future was going to be for Lucas if you and Bode didn't start co-parenting your son immediately. And directly counter some of the ugly public assertions that have been made that insinuate Bode does not care about Lucas. When clearly—" Gannon gave an affable shrug "—of course he does."

Lily wrenched her wrist from Gannon's grip. She shoved her chair back and stalked away from the conference table. Though not one to ever condone violence, she wanted to slug him. "Whose side are you on?" she demanded emotionally.

The uncomfortable silence between them lengthened.

His regard softened slightly. "Yours."

Lily scoffed and planted her hands on her hips. She felt as if she was suffocating in her trim red suit and heels. "It doesn't sound like it!" she said.

He stood and walked around the table to her side. "Just giving you a taste of what the other side is likely to hurl at you."

Was that a hint of protectiveness she saw on his face? Her attorney radar on full alert, she drew in a quavering breath, quipped, "Making sure I'm tough enough?"

Gannon slid his hand beneath her chin, and her heart pounded at the warm assessment in his eyes.

"You're the toughest woman I know," he said gruffly.

Their gazes locked, the moment drew out and Lily's imagination ran wild. Her nipples tightening, she wondered. Was this what it would be like if they ever did kiss—with the air around them charged with tension and excitement?

Was it her imagination, or was he feeling the pull of attraction, too?

The darkening of his irises, the faint but unmistakable pause in his breath said yes. The way he abruptly dropped his hand and stepped back said no. Not yet. Not here and now, with so very much at stake.

All business once again, Gannon slid her a steely look. Warned softly, "It's going to be a bumpy ride unless you can get your emotions under control."

His seemed locked up tighter than a drum.

Lily worked to slow her racing pulse. Her knees suddenly felt a little wobbly, so she leaned against the wall and folded her arms in front of her.

This wasn't like her.

It had to be the threatening crisis that had her wanting him—and the stark masculine protection he offered—so badly.

"Meaning I can't spout off like that in court."

He followed her to the windows that overlooked Main Street. "Or any time you're dealing with your ex, or anyone associated with Bode, for that matter."

Another tense silence fell.

Gannon studied her for another long beat, then gave her a slow, steadfast smile, the kind that said that as long as she let him call the shots, everything would be all right.

Vowing that she was not going to be one of those women who turned to her lawyer for personal comfort, Lily closed her eyes. Swallowed. Instructed herself to use every ounce of common sense and treat him like the extraordinary lawyer he was, nothing more.

Recognizing that it would be a mistake to lean on him in a more intimate way, she opened her eyes, returned to the conference table and pointed to the sheaf of papers she had been served that very morning. "Back to the request for a modification to our custody order." She forced herself to sit down calmly once again. "What's our battle plan?"

"I've already filed a request, asking for an extension. If we're granted it—and we should be—that will give Liz roughly forty days to file an answer. I am also going to file a motion for dismissal this afternoon."

"You think we'll get it?"

"Probably not. But it will send a clear signal to Bode's attorneys that you intend to fight this with everything you've got. Given everything else he has going on career-wise, that alone may give him pause."

Deciding everything was well in hand, Lily reached for her bag. She had to get out of here before things turned even more personal. "You'll let me know?"

He nodded. "One way or another, as soon as I hear. But that likely won't be until early next week."

Which meant she'd be spending the weekend wondering and worrying, Lily realized unhappily.

Knowing she'd spent way too much time alone with Gannon in any case, she said sincerely, "Thanks for all your help." Then made her way for the door.

Lily spent the rest of the day dealing with the fallout over the "fire statue" and working on putting together a weekend work schedule for the upcoming chili festival.

By the time four o'clock rolled around, she was exhausted and ready to call it a day. And that was, of course, when Gannon walked in. She hadn't expected to come face-to-face with him again today, but truth be told, he was a welcome distraction.

He was still wearing the nicely pressed shirt, tweed wool

sport coat and dark jeans he'd had on earlier. She was just as drawn to him now as she'd been before, and in the fading wintry light in her office, she could once again see the inherent protectiveness in his midnight-blue eyes. Except now his dark brown hair was rumpled—as if he'd been running his fingers through the thick, touchable strands. And the hint of evening beard lined his strong, stubborn jaw, further adding to his masculine allure.

Just looking at him made her quiver deep inside.

Oblivious to the sensual nature of her thoughts, he ambled closer and handed her the papers, their fingers touching briefly in the process. "I thought you might like to see a copy of the motion for dismissal for your own files."

She did, but…seeing him again so soon, being alone with him, was something else entirely. Wishing she weren't so attracted to him, she swallowed to ease the parched feeling in her throat. "You could have emailed it to me…via attachment."

The corners of his lips twitched at the exaggerated lack of enthusiasm in her voice. He stepped closer, his eyes heavy lidded and sexy. Smiled. "I wanted to see how you were doing."

Better. Since you walked in the door…

Lily pushed the unwanted emotion away. She stiffened her spine. "I'm fine, as you can see."

And she did not need his protection.

She did, however, temporarily need his legal help. Heart racing, she flipped through the brief. His legal rebuttal was just as she expected—concise and hard-hitting. She sighed in relief. "Looks good."

He flashed a wry smile. "Thanks."

Unsure whether it was the long-simmering, never-acted-on attraction or nerves from all the turmoil of the day causing the butterflies in her midriff, Lily took the document back to her desk and dropped it into her briefcase. She turned back to him, all business now. "So you're all done with your part in my case?" Which meant they'd no longer need to see each other. At least in that regard.

He gave her a long, thorough once-over, then returned his gaze to her face. "Unless Liz needs me again, but yeah, you can consider me officially off the clock."

"Speaking of fees…" She dreaded calculating his hourly rate—which was bound to be exorbitant—times the six or so hours spent. "What do I owe you?"

His hand stopped hers before she could open her checkbook. "Nothing. I work for Liz."

Trying not to notice how the width of his shoulders blocked out the fading winter sunlight, she eased away from his touch. Although the morning had been sunny and clear—almost warm—the weather had shifted again, bringing in cooler temperatures and dismal gray skies. Trying not to feel as depressed as the vista encouraged her to be, she tilted her chin and continued, "Then what do I owe Liz on your behalf?"

He spread his palms and remained maddeningly aloof. "Nothing."

Trying not to wonder if the rest of him was as big and capable as his hands, she gave him a look. Waited.

He shrugged again. "I'm doing this pro bono."

Charity? He was doing this as a charity case? Anger warred with pride. It was true, her salary as mayor wasn't much, but she didn't need much since she had accrued some savings before running for public office. "I don't need your professional largesse, Gannon."

A contemplative silence fell. He gave her a slow, reckless smile that quickly set her heart to pounding. "You really want to pay me back for my help?"

Talk about a loaded question! She regarded him matter-of-factly, letting him know with a glance she did not want to owe him any other favors, either. "Absolutely," she snapped. "The sooner the better."

He edged closer, inundating her with the sandalwood and

spice scent of his cologne and the brisk, masculine fragrance unique to him. "Then how about dinner—tonight?"

Lily blinked. "Are you for real?"

Another slow, seductive smile. "Very."

She drew a quavering breath, held up a staying hand and reminded herself all the reasons why not. "We went through this eight years ago. I'm not going to date you, Gannon."

He comically palmed his chest, as if he'd received a major blow to his heart. Or was it his ego? she wondered. Then he frowned at her in reproof, adding wryly, "I wasn't asking for a date, Lily. I was asking if you wanted to go out to dinner with me." He waggled his brows mischievously. "But... if you want to *call* it a date..."

Lily flushed in embarrassment, as he had obviously meant her to. "I don't," she responded. Pausing, she narrowed her eyes at him. "And I can't have dinner with you because when I'm not working, I'm with my son."

"No problem," Gannon said, not the least bit discouraged. "We can take Lucas with us."

Without warning, she felt an intimacy she didn't expect welling up between them. Most of the men she met viewed the fact she had a child as a major deterrent. Not Gannon. "You really are serious about this."

His lips took on a sober slant. He stepped closer. "I'd like to get to know your son—and I need to talk to you."

Lily's pulse raced at the gentle undertone in his low voice. "About?"

Their eyes met, and Gannon regarded her seriously. "Becoming friends again."

Just the thought of that, Gannon noted in disappointment, was enough to cause Lily to take a step back, away from him.

She held up a delicate left hand, conspicuous only for its lack of wedding and engagement rings. "That's not really necessary, Gannon," she told him archly.

"So you're saying you forgive me for the things I said after we graduated from law school?" When they had still technically been friends. Although he had never stopped wanting something more…

Lily raked her teeth across her soft lower lip. "You were right about Bode, Gannon. He was all wrong for me."

The knowledge brought Gannon no comfort. He followed her back over to her desk. "You didn't think so at the time. In fact, as I recall, you accused me of being jealous of what you had with him."

She shot him an uncompromising look. "Weren't you?"

More like worried. Because Gannon had seen, even when Bode was merely a backup quarterback who'd spent his first three years in the NFL sitting on the bench, that he wasn't the kind of guy who would ever give Lily even a fraction of the love and attention she deserved. A hunch that Bode had proved true shortly after he became a star.

Because then he had dumped Lily. Pronto. And hadn't cared that she had been pregnant with his child.

But seeing no reason to go into that—Lily had suffered enough humiliation due to her ill-considered end-of-law-school liaison with Bode Daniels as it was—Gannon merely folded his arms across his chest. Stood, legs braced apart. "I never stopped wanting to date you."

Lily looked surprised. As if she had never known he had wanted to be anything more than friends after she had rebuffed his advances that first year at UT Law.

Figuring it was time they cleared the air, Gannon went on, "But, by the same token, I wasn't going to waste three years waiting to see if you would change your mind and eventually go out with me after all."

Frustration and regret crossed Lily's face. She held out her hands beseechingly, came closer. "Had I not been in my very first year of law school when you asked me out…had I not seen all of our friends who got seriously involved or married to someone in their first grueling year of professional school eventually have their relationships destroyed amidst all the stress and pressure, I probably would have gone out with you."

"But you didn't want to risk it."

She started to speak. Stopped. Then tried again. An invisible emotional wall went up. "I wanted you to be friends with me, the way we never had been when we were growing up."

"And I was." Although, given how much he had yearned to make her his woman, it had been hard as hell keeping things light.

Her eyes grew stormy. "I wanted us to use that first year to build a foundation for whatever came next, assuming something came next, not just jump heart-first into an affair that was pretty much guaranteed because of the pressure-filled circumstances we were in, as first-years, to crash and burn!"

"You see, Lily?" Gannon shot back. "That's the difference between us. Because I never thought a relationship between us would end in failure. And if you had been brave enough to start something with me, regardless of the timing, you would have discovered what I already knew—that we would have been the exception to the rule. The couple everyone else looked up to because we had made our relationship work in the face of impossible odds."

Briefly, Lily looked as crushed as he had felt back then, when she had turned him down. As though her heart had been broken.

As usual, however, she bounced back fast.

With an angry sniff, she folded her arms in front of her and asserted, "Not that we ever had a chance to find out, since you went on to pursue everything in a skirt that came your way over the next three years. Thereby unwittingly proving my point that relationships forged in the maelstrom of professional school do not last."

Acutely aware his serial dating had been a mistake, embarked on because he was still smarting from Lily's rejection, and knew she would never do anything more than hold him at arm's length, no matter what she said, Gannon shrugged.

"So sue me for not wanting to sit on the sidelines while you soldiered on bravely alone!" Gannon volleyed back. Because, true to her self-flagellating vow, Lily hadn't dated anyone until the very last few weeks of her law school years.

Lily stuffed papers in her briefcase willy-nilly. "You always were an all-or-nothing kind of guy."

His gaze swept over her, head to toe. Reminding him all over again what a lithe, beautiful body she had. How she was determined to let the satisfaction he could bring her go untested. "Whereas you live your life in all half measures," he retorted just as stubbornly.

"You're right. I do see the value in compromise." Lily zipped her briefcase shut with quick, jerky motions. Hunted around for her purse.

Finally finding it, she flung it on her desk next to her briefcase, then defiantly marched toward him, chiding him all the way. "And if you'd grown up the way I had, as the fifth-born of six daughters, you, too, would be happy to get whatever you could—whenever you could—and never ever expect too much because…"

Recognizing another We Can't Do This speech coming on, Gannon decided the time for treating her with kid gloves had passed. Lily was all woman. He was all man. And the attraction between them was tantalizingly real.

Wordlessly, he closed the remaining distance between them and took her in his arms. Flattened one palm over her spine and threaded his other hand through her hair.

Smiling at her gasp of surprise, he tilted her head up, lowered his mouth slowly and deliberately over hers.

"What are you doing?" Lily sputtered, her turquoise eyes flashing.

Just this once, Gannon decided to stop putting his own wants and needs aside. "Showing you exactly what you could expect if you ever let down your guard with me."

Chapter Four

Lily saw the kiss coming. Knew she could have prevented it simply by flattening a hand over Gannon's broad chest. But she didn't push him away. Didn't do anything to keep his head from lowering, ever so deliberately, to hers.

She had dreamed of this moment for years. Yearned for it. Been afraid of it. And the sensation of his lips and body pressed against hers was, she quickly found out, everything she had ever worried and wanted and dreamed it would be.

He was just so darn hard and warm and strong. All over. So tall. So comforting. So alluring.

He tasted good, too. Like mint and man. And desire.

And, oh, sweet heaven, she wanted him in that instant more than she had ever wanted anything or anyone in her life. Which was why she knew she had to end this now.

Hands against his chest, she pushed.

He lifted his head, as she knew he would.

If there was one thing Gannon was to the core, it was a Texas gentleman.

"See?" he teased, sifting a hand through her hair. "That wasn't so bad, now, was it?"

Bad! It had been artful. Seductive. And enthralling. It was all she could do not to groan out loud. Lily gathered her wits and pushed the rest of the way away from him. "I never said I wasn't attracted to you."

He caught her about the waist and reeled her back to him.

Ran a hand lovingly over her spine, eliciting new tingles of awareness everywhere he touched. "Good to hear," he said gruffly, grinning at her prickly manner. "Because I never said that, either." His hot gaze skimmed her face. "In fact, just the opposite is true."

His stubborn words mirrored her own wistful feelings. Which was why she had to be practical. "And that's exactly why we can't take this any farther than we have." His eyes narrowed in response, but Lily forged on. "My life is here. Yours is in Fort Worth. I have a son. You love living the bachelor life." If that wasn't enough to make them put on the brakes, she didn't know what was!

Deep grooves formed on either side of his mouth, and he studied her grimly. "You have it all figured out, don't you?"

Lily drew a bolstering breath. "I don't want to get hurt again, Gannon. The biggest mistake of my life was starting something with someone who I was never destined to be with."

The mention of her former lover was enough to throw a bucket of cold water on his desire. "Bode," he said, letting her go.

Lily nodded sadly. Figuring she might as well tell him the truth about this, she looked him in the eye and admitted, "It wasn't just you who had reservations from the get-go." She pressed a thumb to her sternum. "I knew I wasn't meant for him, any more than Bode was meant to be with me."

A muscle worked in Gannon's jaw. "Then why did you embark on a whirlwind affair with him?"

A hard question that deserved an honest answer. "The excitement of it all. I was at the end of my law school years. Thirty-two months of nonstop studying and stress, and the worry over whether or not I would pass the bar exam and/or get a job upon graduation."

"Which you did," Gannon reminded her.

"Yes, but at that time, I was so overwhelmed. It all seemed like an impossible quest."

He stepped behind her and kneaded the tense muscles of her neck and shoulders. "You should have come to me."

His touch was heaven. Lily melted into it. Closing her eyes, she reminded him softly, "You weren't available. I think you were dating Melinda. Or was it Cassandra—or Marilyn then?"

He shrugged. "Can't remember."

Lily bit down on an oath. "Exactly."

He stood there, patient and evidently ready to turn back the clock again. "Those relationships weren't important to me."

Lily moved off again, determined not to be another one in his long line of women. "Even more on point," she said, exasperation coloring her low tone. "I have responsibilities now, Gannon." She stepped behind her desk. "I can't afford to get involved with the wrong guy for all the wrong reasons."

He studied her, arms crossed over his broad chest. "So you're offering me what exactly?"

She slayed him with her best don't-mess-with-me look. "The same thing I was offering you before. A good enduring friendship—*if* you want it. And that's all."

GANNON WAS STILL thinking about what Lily had offered him, or rather *not* offered him, the next day, when a disreputable-looking pine-green pickup truck made its way up the lane and parked next to the stable. He smiled as Clint McCulloch, a childhood friend and next-door neighbor, got out and ambled toward him. At six foot four, Clint was an inch taller than Gannon, and athletically fit as ever. Like Gannon, Clint had dated a lot but never come anywhere close to settling down. A fact that frustrated the heck out of the available interested women in his path.

"Heard you were back." Gannon extended a welcoming hand.

Clint shook hands firmly. "For good," he said. "And since you're here, too, at least temporarily, I've got a favor to ask."

Gannon slipped bridles over the heads of the three horses remaining on the ranch. Attached reins. "Name it."

Clint moved back to give him room to work. "I need some volunteers for the pony rides at the chili festival. I saw you're judging on Friday and Saturday evenings, but the kiddie stuff is all being held Saturday morning."

Given Lily's decision to stay as far away from him as possible, at least when it came to any physical encounters, Gannon figured the busier he was, the better. It would help him avoid temptation.

Not that this situation would go on for long. As soon as he wrapped up the sale of the Triple M Ranch land to the development company, he would be headed back to Fort Worth. There, his demanding work as partner in a top-notch law firm would not leave room for much else.

And wasn't that ironic.

In law school, Lily had been all work and no play.

Now she was ready to kick back and enjoy more out of life in the small town where they'd both grown up.

Whereas he was focused only on success, to the elimination of most everything else that was distracting—and pleasurable.

Who would have figured…?

Realizing his friend was still waiting for his answer, he opened the stall doors. "Count me in."

"Thanks." Clint accepted the reins on a mare, then followed Gannon and the other two horses out of the barn to the pasture.

It was a nice February morning. Temperature in the low fifties, sunny, not a cloud in the sky. The kind of day that could make Gannon wish he still lived in the country. Or at least had enough time off to enjoy the great weather, and wide-open Texas ranch land.

They unhooked the reins and stepped back to let the horses move freely about. A chestnut, speckled white and inky black, they were all a beautiful sight.

"Heard you're going to sell to Rex Carter," Clint continued.

Gannon pumped water into the troughs. "The land, maybe—depending on how much he offers and what he plans to do with it. Not the house. My mom is set on keeping that and at least one hundred of the five hundred acres surrounding it." But the rest of the land was his to sell.

Clint studied the unkempt condition of the ranch land, along with the even more overgrown property to the south. "Think you'll regret it somewhere down the line?"

Gannon turned to the man who'd ridden the junior rodeo circuit with him when they were teens, then gone on to become a champion in the adult circuit while Gannon had quit competing altogether and went on to college and law school. "Are we talking about you now—or me?" he ribbed.

Clint's demeanor grew remorseful. "I wish I had held on to the place when my four sisters and I inherited it ten years ago instead of selling it to city folk who let the entire ranch go to seed. And then have to use all my savings and negotiate like the dickens to buy it back."

Gannon slapped him on the shoulder, aware they all had their regrets. His own was chiefly Lily. "Well, it's yours now." And Gannon was happy for his pal.

Clint helped Gannon put out some feed. Then eventually asked, "What about your horses? Are you planning to keep them or are you going to sell them, too?"

That was a tricky question. Gannon exhaled. "I hate to—these three have been part of our family since I was a kid. But on the other hand, although they're being well cared for, they're not being exercised enough. But if you're interested...?"

Clint shrugged. "I could board them for you, if you like. Free of charge—if you'll let me use them in some of the riding and roping lessons I'm planning to give. That way they'd still be yours, and you could still ride them whenever you did come back home."

It was the perfect solution to yet another problem of down-sizing. So why was he hesitating? Why was he once again yearning to saddle up and ride whenever he wanted and thinking about how his life had been in simpler times? He had made his decision about where his future lay. Hadn't he? Was okay with the hefty price extracted from working 24/7?

Clint looked at him.

"Let me mull it over," Gannon said.

In the distance, another vehicle turned into the lane and sped toward the ranch house.

"Expecting someone?" Clint asked.

Gannon caught sight of the satellite dish affixed to the top of the white-and-blue van and swore. Just what he did *not* need.

He wondered if Lily had her hands full, too.

"You HAVE TO get that statue out of the town square," Mary-beth Simmons declared. "Sooner, rather than later!"

Lily looked at the delegation of fifteen community leaders standing on her front porch. Farther down the block, a vehicle came to a halt; a door opened and closed. But from where she was standing, Lily could not see who it was.

Deciding to concentrate on those already there, she lifted a calming hand. "Look, I know it wasn't what we all expected. But I think we ought to give it a chance, maybe—"

Rex Carter interjected angrily, "The entire dedication ceremony, complete with fire, is on YouTube! It's had twenty thousand hits so far! And that's just in one twenty-four hour period."

"It's made our whole town—not to mention the chili festival—out to be a joke!" Sonny Sanderson added. Which was a problem for him and his family, because he'd been hoping his barbecue restaurant would sell a lot of food at the event if attendance was even moderately high. Now that might all be for naught—for all the restaurateurs and food vendors planning to take part.

A familiar low male voice joined in. "It gets even more interesting. A Dallas TV station news crew is interviewing my mother as we speak."

Everyone moved to make way for Gannon Montgomery. He'd thrown a leather jacket over his usual shirt and jeans. With a black Stetson slanted across his brow, he looked sexier than ever.

"Sorry," Oscar Gentry, another retired teacher said. "No disrespect meant for your mother, son."

"But we don't want to see her or her art ridiculed, and the way things are going," Yvonne Gentry, another retired teacher, kindly concurred, "Harriett will be made out to be a laughingstock."

Lily—who'd had no time to pull on a coat herself before meeting with the crowd—searched desperately for a solution. "Maybe if we put up a framed explanation beside it, letting people know it's part sculpture and part performance art—"

Around her, everyone paused, exchanged looks, slowly shook their heads. "It's got to be moved to a less conspicuous place than the town square," Miss Mim insisted.

Emmett Briscoe, oilman and art collector extraordinaire, joined them on the front porch of Lily's Craftsman. Nearing seventy, he was still a big, robust, handsome bear of a man. As well as a community and state leader. "Why not put it at the fairgrounds?" he said. "Where the chili cook-off and festival is going to be held? We can put it behind glass in the exhibition hall, along with the explanation that Lily suggested. And then decide what to do with it once the festival is over."

"Given all the publicity we've already had, festival-goers are going to expect to see it." Lily looked at Gannon for support. "We may as well capitalize on that."

Rex Carter scoffed. "How much money is it going to cost to move it?"

"Since it's just from one place to another, and is only the one sculpture, I'm sure it won't be much," Lily said. At least she hoped that was the case.

More grumbling followed.

"Give me until Monday afternoon to come up with a definite plan," Lily urged.

Marybeth Simmons, the leader of the local PTA, huffed, "Well, see that you keep us informed. All our organizations are relying on the money we hope to raise Valentine's Day weekend to fund our projects for the rest of the year."

"I will." Lily thanked everyone for coming, and slowly the crowd dispersed until it was just Lily and Gannon on her front porch.

Shivering, she decided to take the conversation inside her Craftsman-style bungalow. The downstairs had been remodeled into one large space—living room, kitchen and dining area, with a laundry room, half bath and screened-in porch at the rear. Upstairs, she had two bedrooms and a full bathroom.

"How is your mother doing?" Lily asked, grabbing her heavy red wool shawl-collared sweater and slipping it on over her turtleneck and jeans.

Gannon removed his hat before stepping across the threshold and left it on the coatrack in the foyer. Then he followed her over to the fireplace, looking as tense and frustrated as she felt. "Let's just say she's had lots of phone messages and emails, not all of them complimentary."

Lily poked at the fire already burning in the grate. "I don't think anyone understands it, or what it represents." She slid the poker back into the stand, then turned to face Gannon. "Not the way your mother meant anyway."

He stood, hands braced on his hips, pushing the edges of his jacket back. "Even worse—I don't think my mother cares if they do or they don't," he said.

Deciding she could use a hot beverage, Lily headed for her kitchen. "That is the mark of a true artist."

"Or an eccentric," Gannon countered mildly as he looked around, taking in the comfy denim furniture, distressed wood floors and multicolored area rugs. There were toy bins and books galore, most stored in a built-in shelving system on one wall of the living room, as well as a nice entertainment center, complete with stereo TV and DVD player.

Lily paused, pleased that he seemed to like the cozy but practical interior of her home. Not that it mattered.

"You doubt your mother's talent?" she asked.

Gannon watched Lily fill the teakettle and set it on the stove. Brawny arms folded in front of him, he tilted his head, thinking. "All I know for certain is that I don't want to see my mom hurt by all the controversy."

Lily brought out the tea basket and two mugs, glad they were on the same page. "I don't, either." She chose an apricot-vanilla blend while Gannon selected an English tea, known for its strong but mellow flavor. "But I'm afraid if we do nothing, this situation will snowball into a real travesty." Gannon's gaze narrowed. "Do you think I should ask her to return the commission and withdraw the statue from the chili festival of her own volition?"

"I admit that would solve a lot of problems for me and the town immediately."

Gannon took off his jacket and looped it over the back of one of the high stools against the granite-topped island. "But…?" he asked, as he sat down.

Finding the sudden intimacy of the situation a little too intense, Lily turned her eyes to the pale blue walls of her kitchen, then admitted, "I worry what even the *suggestion* she take back her art would do to your mom."

"Well, she won't be happy about it…that's for sure."

As their gazes met again, Lily forged on, "And correct me if I'm wrong, but I understand this was your mother's first serious work. It was a huge honor to even be asked by the town to do this, so to then have it poorly received and hidden away…" She shook her head, barely able to say the words, yet Gannon's expression remained courtroom inscrutable. "Come on, even you, Mr. I'll-Never-Compromise-Under-Any-Situation, can see that's no solution to the dilemma!" she finished emotionally.

Sighing, Gannon shoved a hand through his hair. "You're right about that. My mother's art is every bit as important to her as my career is to me. She waited a long time to be able to pursue it the way she has always wanted to—with all her heart and soul."

Gannon sobered even more. "I don't want to see her pushed into putting her dreams on hold by the people around her any more than I would want to give up my own quest for success."

Reminded of how truly ambitious both Montgomerys were at heart, Lily said quietly, "I don't, either."

Gannon moved closer, his expression intent.

"Then what is the solution?"

"I don't know," Lily said quietly, her heart kicking into a faster beat. She moved to the other side of the counter as the teakettle began to whistle. "But I'm sure if we take a few days to think about it, we'll come up with something a heck of a lot better than what you've just suggested."

His gaze still locked with hers, he flashed a crooked smile. "I'm all for a better solution." He watched her add hot water to the mugs, then rummage around for cookies. "Speaking of family, is Lucas okay with all of the commotion this has caused for you personally?"

Touched to find Gannon thinking of the little boy he had yet to actually meet, Lily admitted in relief, "My parents took him to San Angelo for lunch and a movie with just the two of them. Grandparent Saturday, they call it. So luckily, he didn't see any of it."

Lily broke off as Gannon's phone rang. He moved off to answer it. It didn't take long to discern it was about work.

"So that's what you call a vacation?" she asked some fifteen minutes later, having heard him briskly ask for updates on at least half a dozen cases before finally, finally hanging up.

His lips thinned. "I run the family-law department now. I have a lot of responsibility."

She knew that. Respected it. And yet… "What about a life? Do you have that, too, in Forth Worth?"

And why did she care so much?

He shrugged casually. "My life is my work now."

"But don't you want more than that?" she asked before she could stop herself.

Didn't everyone?

At least if they were completely honest?

Gannon favored her with a sexy half smile, seemingly glad the conversation had taken yet another personal detour. "Are you asking me if I'm currently seeing someone?" he teased.

Was she?

He glided treacherously close. "The answer is no. Not yet."

She inhaled the brisk scent of his cologne, felt the warmth emanating from his body. Lily focused on the strong column of his throat. She splayed her hands across his chest and felt the steady beat of his heart beneath her fingertips. "Meaning there's someone you want to go out with?" she ascertained, pushing the envelope even more.

He sifted his hands through her hair and kissed her temple. "Not there." He looked at her steadily, as if putting it all on the line. "Here."

He had no idea how good that sounded. How wonderful it felt to be this close to him. She drew in a breath.

"You're being reckless again." And, oh, so romantic. And though they were wildly attracted to each other, they remained all wrong for each other as anything but friends.

He knew that.

She knew that.

So why did she want him to pursue her again? Why did she want to wrap her arms around him and kiss him, really kiss him, so much?

Her doorbell rang.

"Saved. Again." Gannon chuckled and stepped back. But not for long, Lily knew.

Regretfully, she went to answer the door.

This time it was Liz Cartwright-Anderson on the other side of the portal. Still clad in her vacation clothes, her blond hair piled in a messy knot on top of her head, she looked at Lily, her expression grim.

Whatever was going on, Lily knew it wasn't good.

"BUT BODE CAN'T do that," Lily sputtered, after her family-law attorney had told her what was going on. "Lucas has never spent any time alone with his dad—ever—anywhere," she continued, upset, glad she had asked Gannon to stay to provide additional counsel if needed. "To expect Lucas to go all the way to Bode's home in Dallas and spend the night and half of tomorrow is just ludicrous! He's only four years old, for heaven's sake. He doesn't even know his father!"

Gannon lounged against the foyer wall, hands shoved in the pockets of his jeans. "Has Lucas ever spent an overnight with anyone else?" he asked quietly.

"Well, yes. With my parents, and occasionally one of my sisters."

He regarded her with a matter-of-factness that both disappointed and stung. "Then it won't be an entirely new experience for him."

"Whose side are you on?" Lily accused, not sure why she felt so betrayed, just knowing that she did.

"This is what you agreed to, after all, in the initial custody agreement."

Afraid her knees would no longer support her, Lily sank down onto the sofa. "Only because I was trying to be reasonable and meet him halfway!"

Liz and Gannon exchanged skeptical glances. "And...?" Liz asked as she sat down in a wing chair opposite Lily.

Lily knew what she said was privileged—it would never leave the room. Doing her best to avoid Gannon's lawyerly gaze, she admitted on a reluctant sigh, "I never expected

Bode to actually exercise the right. Which he hasn't, up to now."

Liz handed over the paper copies of the demand letter sent via email. "Well, now he is. And he wants you to have his son at his Dallas home no later than six o'clock tonight."

"And if I don't?" Lily retorted stubbornly before she could stop herself. Although as a lawyer herself, she already knew the answer to that.

Liz confirmed her thoughts. "His attorneys have promised to alert the judge of the violation, and you'll be held in contempt of court. And, with a change in custody arrangements already being requested, I would not advise you to do anything but follow the current custody agreement *to the letter*. Otherwise…" Her voice trailed off.

His dark brows knitting together, Gannon continued grimly, "They will most likely use your noncompliance as a reason for an emergency custody hearing. And given the fact that I happen to know that the judge who's been assigned to hear the case is also a huge Dallas Gladiators fan…"

"Best not to take any chances. If you want to hold on to the rights you have now," Liz agreed.

Because, Lily knew, even a request for a different judge would run the risk of having it all blow up in her face, even more than it already had. "Okay, then, I'll do it," she said tightly, knowing she really had no choice. How she was going to pull it off successfully, however, was something else indeed.

"You okay?" Gannon asked, as soon as Liz had left. Because the truth was, Lily still looked more than a little shell-shocked by this latest turn of events.

She picked up a pillow and threw it onto the sofa with as much force as she could muster. "I want to scream."

He gave her the space she seemed to require. "Don't blame you."

Lily squeezed another pillow with all her might. Finally, she threw it onto a chair with equal fervor. "Cry."

Gannon watched her strip off her shawl-collared sweater and toss it aside, too. "Understandable."

Her face flushed with angry color. "Punch something." He'd never seen her so overwrought or so incredibly passionately beautiful and he edged closer. Then, resisting the urge to draw her near, he looked at the mantel clock instead. "We've got time if you want to blow off a little steam."

Lily blinked. She swung back to face him in a drift of freesia perfume. *"We?"*

He shrugged as if it were no big deal, when they both knew it was. "I figured I'd tag along, since Liz can't go, and I need to head back to Fort Worth anyway for a day or so to check on a few things there." Since things weren't running as smoothly in his absence as he liked.

Lily closed the distance between them, not stopping until they were toe to toe. She stared at him in shock, asked softly, "You'd really do that for me?"

And a hell of a lot more, if you'd let me.

Knowing, however, that this wasn't the time to put the moves on her, he offered, "Seems as though I owe you, given what you're doing to try to protect my mother."

Silence fell.

Slowly but surely, the walls around her heart began to go back up.

Wanting to protect her more than ever, he used the only logic he knew she would accept and put his lawyer hat back on. "You can't really afford not to have someone go with you," he told her reasonably. "And what better sidekick than a lawyer used to battling the scumbag attorneys responsible for such a power play?"

Lily paused. "You think there's going to be trouble?"

Gannon met and held her gaze. "I think, in law, as in life, it's always best to meet a show of force with another show of force. If I'm there, even just as your friend, there's no chance they'll try to use this situation to undermine you further. And/or attempt to pressure you into anything long term in exchange for a temporary gain."

Lily's posture softened in relief. "Actually, I would feel better if you were by our side."

He smiled and reached for his jacket. "Then that settles it." Which meant they both had to get a move on if they were going to be ready to leave in another hour and a half.

"Gannon?"

He turned to face her.

She came toward him once again and squeezed his hand warmly. "Thanks."

"ARE YOU GOING to spend the night with my dad, too?" Lucas asked from his safety seat, for what, Lily thought on an inward sigh, seemed like the thousandth time since they had left Laramie two and a half hours ago.

Glad Gannon had offered to drive—her nerves felt frayed as it was without having to fight the freeway traffic and unfamiliar city interchanges—Lily turned around to smile encouragingly at her son. "No, honey. This is a special time for you and your dad."

Lucas squinted in confusion. "How come?"

"Because he hasn't spent enough time with you recently."

"How come?"

Lily tried not to tense. "Because he was busy playing football." And doing a million other things.

Lucas's lower lip shot out. He hugged his stuffed horse and blanket close. "I don't want to go."

Oh, sweetheart, I know. Pretending not to notice the look of fear in his eyes, Lily smiled again. "I'm sure you'll have fun."

If there was one thing Bode knew, it was how to have fun. Plus, her ex was still half kid himself.

Gannon stopped at the gate surrounding Bode's Dallas mansion. The guard checked IDs and waved them through.

By the time they reached the elegant portico of the sprawling abode, Bode was coming down the steps. A professional photographer and a videographer, obviously hired to document the occasion, both lingered nearby, ready to capture the first precious moment.

Gannon parked. Lily got her son out while he retrieved the overnight bag, from the rear seat of his luxury pickup truck.

"Hey there, sport," Bode said jovially. Lucas turned his head away from his father and hid his face in his stuffed horse and blue security blanket.

"Lily." Bode nodded at her stiffly.

Noticing her ex seemed to think her son's reticence was her fault, Lily nodded back. "Bode."

Gannon returned with the bag. He handed it over to Lucas, then extended his hand.

For a brief moment, Lily thought Bode was not going to return the gesture. But eventually—maybe because there was an audience and cameras nearby, Bode shook hands.

"Montgomery," he growled.

"Daniels," Gannon returned with professional cool.

Clearly, Lily thought, there was no love lost between the two men. Never had been, and judging from the looks of things now, never would be. An awkward silence fell. Lucas maintained his death grip on her hand, his little body pressed to right side. Gannon was to her left, his presence as steady—and reassuring—as ever.

Even so, it was all Lily could do not to say to hell with everything, grab her son, take Gannon's hand in hers and run far, far away.

Away from her past.

And what scarily looked like her future.

The professional photographer and videographer continued taking in the scene.

Thus prompted, Bode hunkered down in front of Lucas, all macho charm, his voice unutterably gentle. "Want to come inside the house and say hello to your little sisters and Viviana?"

Lucas shook his head and did not look up.

Before Bode could say anything more, the front door opened. His sleek, gorgeous Venezuelan wife appeared. In a belly-baring halter top and flowing pants ensemble, she looked every inch the perennially entitled and pissed-off supermodel she was known to be. She stared at Bode, then lifted her hands as if to say, *What are we waiting for?* And with a last long withering look at Lily and a toss of her wavy golden-brown mane, she disappeared back inside. The door slammed behind her.

The photographer looked at Bode expectantly.

Straightening, he took another look at the door his wife had just gone in, then somberly turned back toward Lily. "Maybe it is a little much to just drop the little buddy off," he said finally.

Gee. You think?

Gannon nodded, in support of Bode's conclusion.

Paternal tenderness suddenly in his eyes, Bode looked at Gannon, man-to-man, then turned and gave Lily a beseeching glance. "How about you and Gannon come inside and stay awhile, and see if we can't all work together to get Lucas settled?"

Chapter Five

Lily thought she knew what to expect from the luxurious interior of Bode's multimillion-dollar home. After all, it had been featured in both *Architectural Digest* and *Personalities! Magazine*.

But nothing could have prepared her for what lay inside.

The elegant white sofas in the formal living room had been pushed to the edges of the huge space. In the center were four separate stations—each sporting an elaborate little-boy birthday cake with a number on top—and a heap of gaily wrapped presents. Bunches of balloons added to the festive atmosphere.

A banner proclaimed Welcome Home, Lucas!

Lucas's eyes lit with interest, while Viviana and her two daughters, ages one and three, watched nearby from the arms of their nannies. His complete PR team and Bode's sports-management agent, as well as his attorneys, were also there—this time dressed as if attending a children's birthday party.

Turning on the charm, Bode knelt down in front of Lucas once again. "I know I missed your first four birthdays, champ," he said. "I'm going to make up for that, starting now."

He rose and, seeming to understand that Lucas would not yet take his hand, motioned for the little boy to follow him. "Want to check out the presents?"

Lucas turned to his mother for permission. She nodded. "Go ahead, honey." It would have been cruel to deny him this, when he had already been deprived of so much where his father was concerned.

Lucas handed Lily his blanket and his stuffed horse for safekeeping. And then cautiously made his way over to the bounty.

The next several hours were a blur of gifts, photos, cakes and song. It seemed every cake had to be lit, "Happy Birthday to You" sung again and again—to Lucas's delight. His two little half sisters eventually joined in the joyful melee.

Lucas's normal bedtime came and went. And still he played happily while Lily and Gannon watched the festivities from the sidelines and photo after photo was taken. Some of which were uploaded to Bode's Twitter feed and transmitted, along with a number of carefully crafted seemingly spontaneous messages, from the star quarterback himself.

Eventually, Bode turned to Lily and Gannon.

She knew that was her cue.

Lily rose and, heart breaking, went over to her son. "Lucas?"

He smiled up at her, a train engine clutched in one hand, a caboose in the other. "It's time for Gannon and I to go," Lily said in a calm, cheerful voice. "You want to say goodbye to us?"

Lucas stood. He turned to Gannon. "Bye, Mr. Montgummy."

"Goodbye, Lucas." Gannon knelt down to offer Lucas his hand.

Lucas grinned and shook it enthusiastically.

Lily knelt down, too. For a second, getting a sense of what it would have been like, if she, Gannon and Lucas were a family.

Pushing her wistfulness aside, she smiled with encouragement at her son.

Lucas smiled back. As he had done many times before, he wreathed his arms about her neck. Hugged her fiercely, then let her go, still smiling with the inner contentment of a relaxed and secure child.

Vowing that she, too, would put on an award-worthy performance if it killed her, Lily gave her son one last impossibly jovial hug. "I'll see you tomorrow around lunchtime, okay?"

Lucas grinned. "'Kay, Mommy."

He went back to playing happily with Bode's three-year-old daughter, Caryn.

Gannon rose, and helped Lily to her feet, squeezing her hand imperceptibly and infusing her with warmth and calm.

It's all going to be okay, Lily reassured herself firmly, more glad than ever Gannon had suggested he come with her. Not just as their attorney, but as a family friend. She felt stronger just standing beside him.

Bode walked Lily and Gannon to the door.

Gannon looked to Lily, seeming to recognize that she needed to give a final word of advice. "He needs his stuffed horse and blanket at bedtime," she told her ex, a catch in her voice. "And he likes a story read to him, too."

Bode nodded.

"And although he's had a lot of cake, he hasn't really had any dinner, so…"

Bode cut her off, his impatience with her lack of faith in his parenting coming through loud and clear. "I got it, Lily. Whatever he needs. Plus—" he paused to cast another fond look at the son they shared "—we've got a nanny of his own standing by to help out as needed, too. I promise you, he'll be fine."

Much as Lily hated to admit it, it seemed her son had adapted far more quickly than she had ever imagined he would.

Gannon gave Lily another look. Letting her know that he, too, thought everything was going to be fine. Otherwise, he would have stepped in.

Recognizing any further delays would not make things

any easier, Lily swallowed and turned back to Bode. "You've got my cell number. I'm staying in the area tonight. So..."

"I'll call you if we need anything," Bode promised, really seeming to mean it.

And that, Lily noted, as she and Gannon were ushered out the door, was that.

"You okay?" Gannon said after they had exited the home and driven away.

Compared to what? Lily thought, blinking back tears. She felt as if a semitruck had just driven square through the center of her heart. Aware she was near the breaking point emotionally—which was something she definitely did not want Gannon to see—she sucked in a quavering breath. She looked out the window until she felt she could speak in a calm tone, and sighed with a weariness that came straight from her soul. "You can just take me straight to my hotel."

The corners of his lips lifted. "Sure you want to do that?" His voice was low, comforting.

"Do what?"

He sent her an intuitive glance. "Be alone?"

Actually, no, she did not want to be alone. But what were the alternatives?

"What are you suggesting?" Her breath hitched in her throat.

He stopped at a traffic light and turned to flash her an understanding smile. "Dinner first."

Lily didn't want to think about what might come next. "I'm not sure I can eat." Her stomach was clenched as tight as the rest of her.

Something hot and sensual shimmered in his smile. "Then, it's the perfect time to have me cook for you. If you don't like it, you'll have a great reason to just nibble a little here and there and pretend it's due to an understandable lack of appetite."

His joking made her smile. For a moment, she let herself

imagine what it might be like to make love with him. Not just once, but many, many times. "You're really inviting me to your place?"

"Might be a good time to see how the other half lives."

Romantic notions bubbled up inside her. Suddenly feeling a whole lot feistier, Lily pivoted toward him as much as her seat belt would allow. "Other half?"

He commanded his luxury pickup with a sure, steady hand. "Us city slickers."

She hesitated, curious despite herself.

What would his place be like? Would it—like the vehicle he drove—have any vestiges of the ranch and small town Texas where he'd grown up? Or be city all the way?

"Come on." He waggled his brows, as if sensing she was on the edge. "It'll give you a good chance to vent." He reached over and briefly—playfully—squeezed her knee. "'Cause I know you've got a lot to say about what went down tonight. And who better to spout off to than someone else who was there?"

He had a point. "Okay," Lily relented finally. "But you can't do all the work."

His low chuckle filled the cab. "You're offering to be my sous chef?"

And that was all. No matter how attractive she found him, she was not going to end up in his arms tonight, not even for comfort.

Disguising her desire, she murmured, "Somehow I think the busier I am, the better."

Gannon sobered. "Probably true," he conceded with a commiserating smile. "In the meantime, start venting. And don't hold anything back."

So Lily didn't.

As Gannon drove the freeways connecting Dallas and Fort Worth, she let loose her feelings on everything Bode had done the past few days. From manipulating the terms of their custody agreement to initiate a sleepover to the massive gift presentation and the way he had turned on the charm to lure Lucas in while simultaneously sending out photos of the event via social media and his PR team.

"The worst of it is," Lily lamented when they reached the high-rise condominium building and entered the underground parking garage, "that Bode will probably go right back to ignoring Lucas as soon as he gets what he wants career-wise."

"And maybe he won't," Gannon said quietly as he turned his truck into a reserved space and cut the motor.

Still feeling a little shaken, Lily gratefully reached for Gannon's hand when he came around to the passenger side and helped her out. She gazed up at him, wishing she could lean on him the way she wanted without there being repercussions. She studied his handsome profile. "You really believe that my ex might come through for Lucas?"

Hand to the center of her back, he led her to the elevator and pressed Up. "I believe that your son is a great kid. I've barely had any time to spend with him and I can see that. So it follows that if Bode gets more thoroughly acquainted with Lucas, he will realize it, too."

The doors slid open. Lily entered the elevator first, and Gannon went in after her.

"And in the long run," Lily mused, forcing herself to put her own insecurities aside and be the adult the situation required, "being wanted, accepted and appreciated by his father could only be good for Lucas."

Gannon nodded, respect for her gleaming in his eyes. "It's a heck of a lot better than the alternative," he said firmly.

THERE WAS A gourmet food shop in one of the retail spaces on the first floor of Gannon's building. They stopped by.

In short order, he bought a nice bottle of burgundy, two porterhouse steaks, fresh spinach and raspberries and a decadent-looking carrot cake with cream cheese frosting from their bakery section.

"You do remember I said I wasn't really that hungry?"

"But I am." He gave her a wolfish grin. "It's possible when you smell the food cooking, you will be, too."

Lily wasn't sure what she expected from his abode, since to date she only really knew the cowboy and law student sides of Gannon. Suffice it to say, she was blown away when they finally walked in.

Gannon's loft was the height of urban sophistication. Approximately two thousand square feet, it sported dark wood floors, rough-hewn brick walls and floor-to-ceiling windows that overlooked downtown Fort Worth. The main living area encompassed half of the space and had a combined gourmet kitchen, living and formal dining area. Off that were a cozy book-lined study, a guest room and a master suite—the latter two each with a luxurious private bath.

All the furniture was heavy, masculine. No upholstered pieces. Just wood and leather. A few modern rugs sporting the red, gray and ivory color scheme of the abode.

"Wow," Lily said when they had completed the tour. *"Nice."*

He grinned, evidently proud of the elegant sophisticated décor, and went to unpack the groceries. "Not how you pictured me living, huh?"

Taking a seat on one of the high-backed stools at the granite-topped kitchen island, she rested her face on her hand, watching him move about. "Actually, given how fast and far you've risen in the legal world, it was *exactly* the way I would have pictured you living."

He rinsed the greens and berries and set them in separate colanders to drain.

"In the lap of luxury," she explained at his inquisitive look.

He opened the wine. "Not as cozy as your place."

She sipped from the glass he gave her. "True. Hard to imagine you having a family here."

He flashed another grin her way and turned on the grill in the center of his stove. While it heated, he crushed a few berries in the bottom of a bowl, and then whisked together a vinaigrette with the ease of a man who cooked well and often. "Who said I wanted a family?"

Lily felt a stab of disappointment, as well as surprise. Telling herself this could be the deal breaker she had been expecting to surface all along, she looked him in the eye. "Don't you?"

GANNON HADN'T. But somehow this evening, he had begun to reconsider. He shrugged and seasoned the steaks. "Haven't really had time to think much about it." The meat sizzled as it hit the hot surface.

With a quiet nod, Lily rose, wineglass in hand, and began to roam. Eventually, she ended up at the windows, staring out at the wintry evening.

The city lights beckoned like gleaming jewels against a black velvet backdrop. But most alluring of all was her.

The waves of her honey-blond hair were deliciously rumpled, as if she had just gotten out of bed. The skin on her face was smooth and flawless, her cheeks flushed a delicate pink. The flowered knit dress and rose-colored cardigan she wore molded nicely to her slender curves and made her look feminine and delicate. Her comfortable flats were casual and mom-like, yet still showed off her spectacularly sexy legs.

Wishing the entire day hadn't been so fraught with tension for her, he continued lazily, "The firm requires I bill at least twenty-four hundred client hours a year. More if I wanted to make partner, which I did. And head up the family-law department." Which amounted to more eighty-hour work-weeks than he wanted to think about...

She came closer, and lounged against the counter. "All work and no play?"

He put together the spinach, berries and almonds and tossed it with the vinaigrette. "All work and a lot of play, too." The steaks sizzled as he turned them.

"Ah, right." Lily slid gracefully back onto one of the bar

stools in front of the kitchen island. "You and your legion of girlfriends."

The aroma of grilled meat filled the room. It was enough to make them both salivate.

Gannon brought out the salad plates and silverware, then sat opposite her. "I think you've jumped to the wrong conclusion about that." He paused to look her in the eye. "The vast majority of them were platonic friends."

Lily stabbed a fork into her salad. "What about that flight attendant you dated toward the end of law school? Weren't you with her for a couple of years?"

Satisfaction roared through him as he got up to pull the steaks off the stove. He plated them and brought them back to the counter to let them rest. "You kept up on the gossip about me."

Lily finished her wine and the salad and dug in to the steak. "And you didn't answer the question."

Gannon savored his meal, too.

Recognizing she wasn't going to let this go, he finally refilled both their glasses and said, "Turns out that dating someone while you're studying for the bar and starting a job as a junior associate in a law firm is no more conducive to forging a successful relationship than while you're in law school trying to survive."

Lily made a comically surprised face. "Is that you?" She laid a hand over the soft swell of her breasts. "Conceding I might have been right all along?"

His gaze drifted south. He tried not to think about what she might—or might not—be wearing beneath her clothes. Or how much he wanted and needed to touch.

He finished his steak and pushed his plate away. "In most cases," he agreed. "If you and I had dated when we were in law school, it would have been different."

Soft lips quirking, she studied him, too. Carried her plate to the sink. "You're dreaming."

He caught her by the shoulders, turned her gently to face

him. "And you refuse to dream." Wondering what it would take to get her to lower her defenses, even a little bit, he lifted a challenging brow. "Still…"

She caught her breath and splayed her hands across his chest. He tugged her close anyway, loving the softness of her, the femininity, the warmth.

"Can you blame me?" she asked, clearly not liking the direction the conversation was headed. Though her body was heating from head to toe, she continued to resist what he figured they both knew, deep down, was inevitable.

She bit her lip. "It seems like whenever I let myself hope for something special, I crash and burn."

Tenderness welled inside him. Gannon tucked a strand of hair behind her ear. "Only because you've never hoped for the right things from the right guy."

"Now who's being ridiculously idealistic?" she scoffed.

He lowered his head over hers.

Ignoring her tiny gasp of surprise, he captured her lips. "Me."

THE KISS CAME. Lily knew she should resist. But she couldn't do that this time any more than she had been able to do so the last time he had taken her in his arms. Wreathing her arms about his neck, she opened her mouth to the pressure of his and kissed him back with all the pent-up emotion of the evening.

Not just once, but again and again. She let the tender intensity of his embrace do away with her resistance and speak to the woman inside her.

It didn't matter that she shouldn't be here with him, at his place. Or that she was a sensible woman, whose heart was safely locked up, away from all her previous mistakes.

What mattered was that she had wanted this forever.

Had wanted *him* forever.

Wanted to be held, loved, kissed the way only he seemed able to do. She pressed closer still. Savoring his heat and his strength, the taste of him and the satisfying tangle of their lips and tongues.

He knew how to kiss her, knew how to hold her.

When he tucked an arm beneath her knees and lifted her up into his arms and carried her toward the master bedroom, her pleasure, her want, her need only increased.

Lily felt on the edge of a contentment she had never had and always wanted. She felt as though she could give him the same.

When they finally reached his bed, he let her down gently. Still kissing, they came together again. Undressing each other, piece by piece, between long, lingering kisses filled with pent-up passion and need.

He was hot, hard, big. Cupping her breasts, kissing her, moving his hands lower still with smooth languid strokes. Drawing her down onto her bed. Kindling her senses. Driving her toward wild abandon.

Gannon hadn't expected to make love to Lily tonight. He had expected to spend time with her. Make her feel better, really get to know her all over again—as adults this time. But that was before she had looked at him with such overpowering need. Before she had kissed him and held him and stroked his entire body, hard and soft and every way in between. Before she, too, writhed in ecstasy with each stroke of his hands, lips and tongue. Before she surrendered to him completely, toes curling, keening those soft breathy little cries…

He slid overtop her. She shifted restlessly, opening her legs even more, arching, urging him on, even as she pulled him close. He gripped her hips and slid home, kissing her all the while. Her body quivered in surprise, in pleasure. And then they were lost again, their bodies immersed in friction, in need, in sweet encompassing heat. Her hands rubbed his shoulders, her nipples his chest, lower still, her thighs closed around his hips. Until there was nothing but the intense driving need, giving and surrender.

He couldn't get enough of her.

She couldn't get enough of him.

And maybe, just maybe, Gannon thought as they savored each fierce deliberate thrust and intoxicating kiss and finally catapulted over the edge, this was the way it had always been meant to be.

IT TOOK LILY less than five minutes to come crashing back to reality.

Gannon rolled onto his side and watched her get out of his bed. "Regrets already?"

Lily noted he didn't look surprised. She rummaged around for her underwear. "I used you."

He swung his legs over the edge of the bed. "The last thing you need to be worrying about right now is me, sweetheart."

His gruff, sexy voice made her quiver all over again. Lily trembled as she slipped on her bra and reached around behind her to fasten it. "What are you saying? That you can take care of yourself?"

He strode to her side and deftly engaged the hook-and-eye closure for her. "And then some."

Still naked, he stepped back to admire the sight of her in her pale pink bra and bikini panties.

The depth of his smile and the knowledge she wasn't the only one getting aroused again sent another whisper of shame rushing through her.

She hunted around for her dress. "This wouldn't have happened if I hadn't had such a horrible day."

"Uh-huh." Lazily, he reached for his boxer briefs and tugged them on.

Lily slipped her dress over her head, then shimmied it down the length of her body. "Or if I'd done what we both knew I should have done and headed for my hotel—instead of come here with you."

Once again, Gannon stepped behind her—this time to work the zipper. He peered around her shoulder. "You trying to insinuate I'm a bad chef?"

Lily found one flat but not the other. "You know you're not," she huffed.

He pulled on his jeans but left the fly open. "Lazy about getting the dishes, then…"

She reddened as he gave her a sexy once-over, and tried not to notice just how big and hard and strong he was. *All over.*

She hunted around until she found her other shoe. "Under the circumstances, I can't hold that against you." She sat down on the edge of the bed to put it on.

He came closer, her discarded cardigan in hand. She took it back, then realized it was inside out. "Then…?" Chivalrous as always, he helped her reverse the fabric and slip it on.

Struggling against the need to make love with him again, even more thoroughly this time, Lily stopped abruptly, listened. "Is that my *cell phone*?"

Gannon nodded.

Noting it was past midnight, Lily raced to answer.

Chapter Six

Traffic was light at one o'clock in the morning. But it still took Gannon and Lily a good half hour to get to Bode's estate.

This time the security guard opened the gates on approach and waved them through.

They'd barely stopped the car when the front doors of the mansion flew open and Bode walked out, a tearful Lucas, plus Blue Blankie and his stuffed horse in his arms.

Bode was no more happy to see Gannon than Gannon was to see him, Lily noted.

Not that Gannon—with his devotion to family—would have ever put her and her son in a situation like this in the first place.

"Mommy!" Lucas sobbed.

Lily held out her arms. Lucas vaulted into them and broke into a fresh wave of hiccups.

The nanny hired to care for Lucas stepped out onto the porch, overnight bag in her hand. She handed it over to Gannon, who remained ready to assist Lily—and her son—in any way he could.

"How long has Lucas been like this?" Lily asked, holding her son close and brushing a hand through his hair. She'd known this was a mistake. It didn't help to have her private prediction come true, though.

"Since midnight."

Lily lifted a brow in surprise. Beside her, Gannon seemed equally nonplussed.

Bode tucked his hands beneath his arms. "He and I were having such a good time playing, so I let him stay up late." He paused. "He's really smart, you know?"

Glad his hiccups were subsiding, Lily stroked her son's hair. "I do." Although it was good to hear his biological father recognize that.

Bode inhaled. "Anyway, he started to go to bed okay. He said I needed to read him a story and tuck him in with Blue Blankie and Horse. So I did all that, and then when I went to turn out the light, he suddenly said he wanted to go home to you." There was a long pause. "I said you wouldn't be here to get him until lunchtime tomorrow. He burst into tears. And nothing any of us did or said could comfort him." Bode swallowed, regret sparking briefly on his face. "So I called you," he concluded tersely, then looked her in the eye. "Thanks for coming, by the way."

"Anytime," Lily returned softly, and she meant it. It didn't matter how or why he'd gotten in this situation. If her little boy needed her, she would be there.

Bode gently touched Lucas's shoulder. "Maybe next time you can spend the night, okay, buddy?"

Lucas burst into tears again.

"Or you could do the right thing. Take things slow and give him more of a chance to adjust," Gannon said quietly.

This event had set the father-son relationship back a notch. They all knew that, Lily thought.

Even Bode.

Although, as expected, her ex did not admit to making a mistake.

Instead, Bode gave their son another pat on the shoulder, said goodbye again and then backed up.

Lily looked at Gannon, who seemed more than ready to depart—as was she.

Lily looked in Gannon's eyes. "I'm going to sit in the back with him."

He nodded, understanding. "Absolutely."

Together, they got Lucas into the car booster seat and all buckled in. Lily climbed in after him and put her arm around her little boy. He continued to cry softly, so overtired now he was practically incoherent. As the three of them headed away from Bode's mansion, it was all Lily could do not to burst into tears, too.

GANNON GLANCED AT the mother and son in the backseat of his car via his rearview mirror. "Sure you want to try to check in to a hotel now?" he asked with concern. "You're both welcome to stay at my place in the guest room."

A small silence. Then Lily, the expression on her face sad and defeated, said, "You wouldn't mind?"

"Prefer it." It seemed the better option since Lucas was still so upset. This way he could help if needed, and he wouldn't have to wonder and worry if they were okay.

Lily heaved a big sigh of relief. "Thanks, then."

Gannon continued driving. He found an easy-listening station on the satellite radio that was playing soothing music. By the time they reached the parking garage beneath his building, Lucas was sleeping, his head on his mother's shoulder. It was Lily, Gannon noted, who was now in tears.

Since it was evident she was embarrassed about it, he pretended not to notice as he helped her get Lucas out of the car. She wanted to carry her son herself, so he got their bags from the trunk. Together, they took the elevator up to his loft and brought Lucas into the guest room. Tucked him into bed. Lily stayed with him long enough to make sure he was still asleep, then came out into the living room. She looked at Gannon. "If you don't mind, I'm going to hit the sack, too."

Gannon pressed a hand to her cheek, a kiss to her brow. "You know where to find me if you need anything."

And for that night, anyway, that was that.

IT WAS, AS Lily had expected, one long night. Every forty-five minutes or so, Lucas woke up crying. Never coming all the way to consciousness.

Never entirely letting go of his anguish and confusion.

Lily took him into her arms and cuddled him close. "Hush now, baby, hush…Mommy's here…" she soothed, over and over, until he went back to sleep.

And then, just as she was about to drift off herself, he would wake again and the whole process would start all over.

Until finally, eventually, both of them slept.

Lily woke with the smell of pancakes and fresh-brewed coffee teasing her nose, the sound of male laughter filling her ears.

She sat up with a start, for a moment confused about where she was and how she'd gotten there.

Then she recalled. *Everything.*

Tossing back the covers, she padded in the direction of the laughter. Gannon and Lucas were cuddled together on his leather sofa, eating pancakes and watching the antics of Big Bird and Cookie Monster on Gannon's big-screen TV.

Lucas grinned when he saw her. "Look, Mommy!" He pointed at the television. *"Sesame Street!"*

Gannon grinned. In a T-shirt, jeans and moccasins, hair rumpled, his face unshaven, he looked incredibly sexy. Remembering how they had made love the night before, Lily felt a thrill sweep through her. She wanted to say she regretted it. She didn't—although she did regret using Gannon the way she had. He was too good a man for that. Not that he looked as though he minded.

Smiling, he let his eyes drift over her, too, before meeting her gaze. "Hungry?"

She hadn't been. Until now. Lily glanced at the breakfast the two of them were systematically devouring. "You cooked?"

"The deli downstairs did. I asked them to deliver pancakes, bacon, fresh fruit, juice and milk." He inclined his head modestly. "The coffee I did make myself."

It all smelled incredible. She walked over to the kitchen. On the other side of the counter, the offerings were displayed. "Nice."

"Plates are in the cupboard. Silverware in the drawer. Mugs on the counter next to the coffeepot."

She liked that he could be casual about it. So kind and hospitable.

Lily shook her head as she watched Lucas and Gannon burst into another torrent of laughter over the antics on screen. She joined them on the sofa, plate in hand, Lucas between the adults.

She had a knife and fork. Lucas and Gannon were both eating their hotcakes the guy way, by hand dipping the golden discs into the syrup on their plates.

Funny how much her life had changed in just a few days.

After years of neglect, Bode wanted back into Lucas's life. If only until he got what he wanted, career-wise.

Gannon was back in hers. A heck of a lot more intimately than she had ever expected. And though she had told him the evening before that their lovemaking had been a one-time thing, born out of emotional despair and stress, now she was wondering if that was really true.

One thing was for certain.

She didn't know what she would have done the past few days without him.

"Are you still okay with me stopping by the law firm before we leave town?" Gannon asked Lily several hours later, after they'd both showered and dressed. "It's only going to take a few minutes. But if you want to wait here…"

Lily looked at Lucas. He seemed fine now, sitting on the floor, building a pyramid out of a stack of plastic souvenir beverage cups from various athletic events. She could certainly vouch for her own behavior. But her sleep-deprived son's—after all he'd been through last night—was a different question entirely. It might not take a lot to set him off. On the other hand, because he was with her and Gannon, whom he seemed to like immensely, he might be fine.

"Is anyone else going to be in?"

Gannon shrugged. "Sunday afternoon? Hard to say. Definitely some junior associates. Maybe a few paralegals. Everyone who is there will likely be in jeans."

Sounded casual enough. Still…Lily had to ask. "Is there a lobby we can wait in?"

Gannon grinned, as proudly as he had when he'd shown her his loft. "Actually, I'd like to show you around, if you're up for it."

Lily looked at Lucas with mom-like candor. "Can you behave like a big boy and use your inside voice and your good manners if we go and see where Gannon works?"

Lucas puffed out his chest, suddenly looking important. "Yes," he said.

Lily took her son at his word. The three of them loaded up their belongings in Gannon's car, and headed for downtown. The law firm was located in a skyscraper on West 10th Street. Gannon's firm occupied the entire seventeenth and eighteenth floors. His office was on the eighteenth.

It was, Lily noted, as luxurious as one would expect a big-time Texas law firm to be. With plush carpeting and elegant glass-walled offices. Lots of original art and upscale furnishings. And, as Gannon had predicted, there were a number of junior partners behind their computers, slaving away.

He led the way to his office. It was bigger than a lot of them they had seen thus far, decorated in masculine tones of brown and beige. He gestured affably. "Make yourself at home."

Lily settled Lucas on the sofa and handed him her computer tablet. She cued up a matching game for him to keep him occupied. To her relief, he got quickly into it. Which gave her a chance to look around at the diplomas, bar licenses—

Gannon seemed to have passed the bar exam in New York and California, too—and various awards on his walls.

Aware he was watching her, she turned to face him. "You've done well for yourself."

He grinned with satisfaction. "I have."

A group filed out from the elevator into the vast reception area. An older man, a much younger, incredibly beautiful woman and two others, who, judging by their demeanor, were all firm employees. As they approached, Gannon paused, almost in shock. They nodded officiously at him, a couple of them giving him an almost pitying look, then went down the hall.

Gannon continued looking after them, his body very still.

"Something wrong?" she murmured.

His mouth tightened. He turned to her, his face an inscrutable mask. "Excuse me a minute?" he asked pleasantly.

"Sure." Lily sat down next to Lucas.

Eventually, Gannon returned. He took a stack of mail and a few files, then put them in his briefcase. "Ready?"

Lily nodded.

Gannon said nothing else until they had left downtown and were headed west, out of Fort Worth. But she could tell from his body language that he was still on edge.

"Lunch now or later?" he asked.

Lily cast a glance behind her. Lucas, who rarely took naps these days, was fast asleep in his safety seat. "Later, if it's okay with you."

"Just say when."

Lily nodded. "You know, you don't have to talk to me…"

"I don't?" he asked, raising his brows.

She ignored his attempt to distract her with a joke. "But I can tell something's on your mind."

His expression darkened. "Yeah."

"Something to do with work?"

Emotions still carefully hidden, he slanted her a glance. "You're not going to let it go."

Lily couldn't be sure if that was a good thing in his view or a bad thing. She only knew he needed to talk to somebody about whatever it was that had happened back there.

She shrugged as if it wouldn't matter one way or another, when the truth was, she'd be hurt if he didn't trust her enough to talk to her, at least in generalities. "I've confided in you." She studied his strong, masculine profile, saw him relax ever so slightly. Impulsively she reached over and briefly touched his biceps. "It seems only fair I serve as your sounding board, too."

Gannon caught her hand and lifted it briefly to his lips, then he kissed the inside of her wrist before letting her go once again.

"The group of employees we saw back at the office was there to work on a specific case." He sped up to merge onto the freeway. "The client—who wasn't there today—is about to enter into his fifth marriage. I was tasked with drawing up the happy couple's prenuptial agreement. I balked. And it seems they went ahead without me."

And apparently hadn't told him, either. "Why?"

Gannon's jaw clenched. "Let's just say I didn't feel good about the way the groom wanted it done."

With effort, Lily resisted the urge to touch him again. To physically comfort him just like he'd done for her. "Fast and dirty?"

His disappointment fading, he flashed her a rueful smile. "How did you know?"

The traffic thinned as they headed away from the city. Lily relaxed back in her seat. "So what was the scheme?"

"There was to be only one legal team of his lawyers."

"Why didn't she have representation?"

Gannon exhaled. "Our client said if she needed her own lawyers, she didn't need to be married to him."

That sounded like a man more attached to his money than the woman he was about to marry. "What does the prenup stipulate?"

Gannon's gaze narrowed. "That she will get nothing if and when they do divorce."

"And they likely will."

A brief nod of his head. "Experience says before she's thirty, if not sooner." His voice dropped another disgruntled notch. "His brides tend to have an expiration date."

"Maybe you lucked out, then, not having to draft the pre-nup." Lily studied the tense set of his broad shoulders. "But clearly you don't see it that way."

His expression didn't change in the slightest. Yet there was something in his eyes. Some small glimmer of frustration. "It's a black mark against me. And the hell of it is, the managing partners are right." He shook his head in grim self-reproach. "I'm paid to do a job, and that's represent my client, protect his or her interests—*not* worry about everyone or anyone else."

"But you do." And she loved that about him, whether he saw it as an asset or not.

He sighed heavily. "The bane of being brought up in a small town, I guess. Everyone looks out after everyone else."

Maybe they didn't live in such different universes after all. Lily smiled, feeling in sync with him yet again. "It's all about neighbor helping neighbor," she agreed. "Not about how many billable hours you can accrue. Or how many clients you can bring in."

He passed a slow-moving truck, then got back into the right lane. "Which brings me to my next question. Why aren't you practicing law?"

The curiosity in his low, intimate tone sent heat shimmying through her. Realizing her skirt had ridden up her thigh, she tugged it back down again. "I hated the adversarial nature of litigation. The mind-set, more often than not, that there had to be winners and losers instead of all winners."

He grinned in a way that reminded her he had always felt she was far too softhearted for her own good. "So you went into politics instead?"

His voice was soft and rough, the way it had been when they were in bed. Lily swallowed around the sudden tightness of her throat and turned her gaze from his handsome profile to the passing scenery. "Rex Carter is great at bringing in new business, growing the community that way, but he's not so great at providing funds for the existing infrastructure and all the organizations that make Laramie the friendly, warm and welcoming, down-home community it is."

"So you stepped up."

She drew a deep breath as she took in the flat, sagebrush-dotted land and the occasional herd of cattle or horses. In control of her emotions once again, she turned back to Gannon and answered candidly, "At least for a while."

He tossed her another quick, interested look. One that compelled her to admit, "Don't tell anyone, but...there's a lot about politics I hate."

To her relief, he wasn't as shocked as she would have figured.

"The fire statue was more than you could take?" he deadpanned.

Lily laughed despite herself. "Funny. No." She cast a look over her shoulder to make sure her son was still asleep. "I just... I'm not sure I'm cut out to be a politician for the rest of my life, either. I mean, I like working for the greater good and helping the community, but a lot of the minutiae—the petitions, and so on—are enough to drive me up a wall, and it's only been a little over three years now." Come May, she'd have to make the decision whether to run for office again or simply finish out her term in November and move on.

Gannon smiled. "Some of that would exasperate me, too."

Lily appreciated the empathy. Unfortunately, all the shifting around had caused her skirt to ride up again, and this time, to her chagrin, Gannon had definitely noticed. Blushing, she tugged it down and pressed her knees together primly.

He lifted a brow, obviously appreciating the view but too

much of a gentleman to comment, then turned their attention back to the conversation. "Any idea what you want to do if you don't continue in politics?" he asked sincerely.

Relieved to think about something other than the continual sexual sparks between them and the very real possibility of making love with him again, Lily pulled herself together and replied, "Honestly? I don't know. I might go back to the law in some shape or form that includes some sort of problem solving."

He nodded in something akin to approval.

She shrugged, a little embarrassed by how vague and uncertain she sounded. "Luckily, I've got time to figure it out," Lily said. "And a job to do in the meantime."

Which, given all she had to do before the advent of the chili cook-off and festival the following weekend, would keep her so busy she wouldn't have the time or the energy to get any more involved with Gannon.

And that, she knew, given how different they still were, could only be a good thing.

She had rushed into a relationship once, with Lucas's biological father, and that had turned out to be a huge mistake. She wasn't going to let herself do it again.

"Is that everything?" Gannon asked, an hour and a half later after carrying their overnight bags inside for her. Lily had been cordial but pensive for the last part of the drive. He sensed she had a lot on her mind and might need to unburden herself again—out of earshot of her little boy.

Lily watched her son, who was invigorated after his long nap in the car, make a run for his building blocks and collection of toy ranch animals. "I think so," she replied, visually checking over their belongings, including Lucas's treasured Blue Blankie and stuffed horse, both of which were under his arm.

Not eager to leave, especially when she still seemed to be

a little out of sorts, Gannon asked casually, "Any thoughts about what you're going to do for linner?"

As hoped, his teasing tone coaxed a smile from her. *"Linner?"*

He regarded her with mock solemnity. "Lunch and dinner. Sort of like brunch."

They never had stopped to get anything to eat en route for fear of waking her son. He was starved, and he figured she and Lucas had to be hungry, too.

She waved desultorily. "We'll probably just have a snack and I'll make an early dinner."

Or, in other words, she was not asking him to stay.

Lily drew a deep breath. She took him by the wrist and led him deeper into the kitchen, out of earshot of her son. Looking deep into his eyes, she said quietly, "I know that the past twenty-four hours have been really intense. And that I've leaned on you in an unconscionable way."

Sensing a breakup speech coming on, not unlike the We Can't Do This Now—Or Ever! talk she had given him during their first year of law school, Gannon shot back, "Is that what you call what happened between us last night?" He kept his voice mild with effort. "Unconscionable?"

Bright spots of color appeared in her cheeks. She lowered her glance self-consciously, whispering, "I was not myself. You know that."

If he truly thought that, he would have felt like the worst kind of user. "Or maybe you were yourself," he countered softly, taking the opposite tact. Hand to her chin, he lifted her face to his. "And just don't like what you discovered."

Defiantly, Lily held his gaze. "That being?"

"The chemistry we have."

She drew a sharp breath. "I never denied..."

"Wanting me?" He stared into her eyes for a long, heated moment, then dropped his hand.

Her lower lip trembled. "It's always been a question of timing."

"Which is never right," he said, feeling another sucker punch coming on.

"Please understand." She gripped his forearms. "I never meant to hurt you."

He exhaled roughly. "Well, that sure makes all the difference."

On the verge of tears, she pleaded, "Can't we just go back to being friends?"

Here was his chance. To save himself from another round of heartbreak and humiliation at her hands and sever ties, too. Only that wasn't what he wanted, either. "Friends," he repeated, trying to figure out if that would ever suffice.

Lily nodded, eager to make peace. "Former law school buddies. Colleagues in the legal profession. Neighbors."

Even as she spoke, it all sounded so lame. Had she not been through so much in the past few days thanks to her jerk of an ex, Gannon would have told her to hell with half measures, to hell with pretending that they didn't feel what they did. Because the truth was, they could have a shot at something real here—if they just allowed themselves to go forward, unhampered by fear of making yet another mistake in the romantic department.

But she had been through a lot.

So had her son.

Which was why he could not walk away. Not at this moment anyway. Even if it meant he was now the fool.

Realizing a lighter tone was called for, however, he teased, "Does this mean you won't be my valentine?"

Lily groaned and pressed her fingertips to her temples. "I'm not going to be anyone's valentine, Gannon. Now or ever."

Knowing he still had another seven days to change her mind about the two of them remaining lovers—and more—Gannon smiled. "So noted."

Chapter Seven

Lily woke Monday morning wondering if she had made a mistake in telling Gannon she wasn't prepared to be anything more than casual friends—or an occasional lover—with any man.

He had taken it well.

Too well.

Promising cheerfully before he'd left her home to touch base with her in a day or so to see how things were going.

Which could have meant anything.

An email. A call. An unexpected visit.

She hadn't nailed him down because that would have meant she was interested in him romantically.

Which, deep down inside, she knew that she was.

She also knew all the reasons why it wouldn't work. Gannon was "all in" his work in Fort Worth, to the point he didn't even have time to date anyone these days. The only reason he had time to pursue her was because he was in Laramie to support his mother and see to the sale of the family ranchland. Once Gannon achieved those two things, he would return to his ultrasophisticated life in the city.

Her experience with Bode and the press had left her wanting to be as far from the limelight as possible. She was focused on raising her son, and wanted to be in Laramie near family and friends. Career was now secondary to her. Career was everything to him.

Plus, once his "vacation" was over in a few days, he would be gone.

Which was why she had to stay strong. Remain independent. And most important of all, make damn sure that she and Gannon never hurt each other again.

So she pulled herself together, had breakfast with her son—who seemed to have recovered admirably from the confusing events of the weekend—then dropped him off at school and headed for town hall to tackle her own massive to-do list.

Unfortunately, she had just settled down to work when her attorney called. "We've had some new developments in the case."

That was fast, Lily thought. But given her ex's superstar status and high-profile Dallas legal team, perhaps not surprising. Connections weren't *supposed* to make a difference when it came to the fair application of the law, but somehow they always did.

"I'd like Gannon to sit in on our meeting, if it's okay with you," Liz continued.

Actually, it was more than okay. Although it was not her style to want a man to protect her, having Gannon by her side always made her feel better. He was a top Dallas–Fort Worth area attorney, too. Keeping him on their team, even in a consulting capacity, would make the legal battle more equitable. "That'd be great," she enthused.

"Can you be in my office at ten-thirty?" Liz continued, sounding happy they were on the same page. "It shouldn't take long."

By the time Lily arrived, Gannon and Liz were setting up in the conference room. She could tell from the sober expressions on both their faces the news was mixed, at best.

"We heard back from the court," Liz said, getting right down to business. "The request for dismissal was denied. The judge felt enough time had elapsed from the initial hearings on custody to warrant a fresh look at the arrangements. But the twenty-day extension to file our answer to their complaint *was* granted."

Which meant, Lily thought, putting on her lawyer hat, too, they had another thirty-seven days to formally respond. And by then, Bode might well have a new contract with the Dallas Gladiators. Hence ending his need for the image rehabilitation and PR blitz.

The attorney continued, "Meantime, both parties have been ordered to mediation."

Lily turned to Gannon. He was in country lawyer garb— olive green corduroy sport coat, open-necked white shirt, dark jeans, boots—looking handsome as could be. He smelled good, too, like sandalwood and spice. Just looking at him made her remember how it had felt to make love with him, how good it always felt whenever he was by her side.

With effort, Lily turned her attention back to the situation they were there to discuss. "I was hoping, after the way things went Saturday evening, Bode would have already instructed his lawyers to drop the custody suit."

"Tell me about the visit." Liz began to take notes.

With Gannon wordlessly encouraging her, Lily related everything from the awkward reunion of father and son to the over-the-top birthday party and multitude of gifts for all the yearly milestones he'd missed. The fact that, while Bode had been doing his best to forge a genuine connection with his son and make them all comfortable, his PR team had been busy spinning the event and Tweeting out photos.

"Yeah, I saw some of them," Liz said ruefully. "They were on a number of celebrity blogs." A devoted mother herself, she did not look impressed. She continued writing. "We can use that against him if we need to."

Gannon agreed, "Judges hate seeing kids used as pawns."

"So you were comfortable leaving Lucas there for the night?" Liz asked.

Lily nodded. "He seemed as if he was going to be fine."

Only he hadn't been. She finished with her son's postmidnight meltdown.

Liz tapped her pen thoughtfully against her chin. "What was Bode's reaction to this?"

Lily looked at Gannon. "Actually, pretty commendable, wouldn't you say?"

He nodded. "Bode did the right thing for Lucas, actually for everyone, in calling Lily to come and get Lucas."

Lily turned back to the other woman. "Do you think his attorneys know about this?"

Liz nodded. "I'm sure they checked in with him, then advised Bode to look at the long game and take the next steps as planned."

Overwrought with emotion, Lily took a deep breath. She wished she could reach over and hold Gannon's hand but, knowing how inappropriate that would be under the circumstances, remained where she was. "Is there any way to delay mediation? Maybe give Bode more of a chance to reconsider?" As she was *still* sure her ex would, once his contract negotiations were settled.

Liz and Gannon shook their heads in unison. "The opposing attorneys have already suggested Ted Mackey for February 13—"

Lily lifted a staying palm. "That's the first day of the chili festival. So I can't be in Dallas then. I have to be here."

Liz made another note. "So we'll change the date for after the festival. What about that mediator?" Liz turned to Gannon. "Know anything about him?"

Gannon nodded. "Mackey is a big proponent of having both parents in children's lives whenever possible, but statistically, he's known to side with dads more than moms."

Liz crossed Mackey off the list. "The second option is Darla Royce."

"She's extremely thorough in her investigations, which means nothing will get by her." Gannon paused, thinking.

"She also usually makes contentious situations even more combative."

Liz axed Royce, too. "The last and third option they offered is Benjamin Cohen."

Gannon shook his head. "Sincere, but he's only been at this a few years and can be easily swayed to one side, then the other, so you never know what he's going to suggest as a solution."

Sighing in frustration, Liz marked Cohen off, too. "Who would you suggest, then?"

Gannon's reply was firm. "Starr Calder is the best mediator in the Dallas–Fort Worth area. She's always fair. Creative in her solutions. The only downside—if she has one—is that she has a long waiting list of people wanting to see her." He cleared his throat. "But on the upside, judges usually like getting her involved in a case because, more often than not, problems are settled quickly in her office. And never make it to court."

That sounded good to Lily, too.

"I'll call her, and opposing counsel, now." Liz left the room.

For the first time since she'd entered the office, Lily and Gannon were alone.

He reached across the table and lightly touched her forearm with the same tenderness he'd made love to her. His gaze drifted over her face. "You doing okay?"

Tingling everywhere they'd touched—and everywhere they hadn't—Lily forced a tremulous smile. "Yes, I'm just frazzled."

In the past five days, her life had taken a turn that seemed slightly surreal. Amplified by the fact that it had barely been a day since she and Gannon had seen each other and it already seemed way too long.

Which was crazy, since she had never been the type to let herself depend on a man.

Gannon squeezed her palm before he let her go. "Just so

you know," he said in a husky voice, "I'm here for you in any capacity needed."

Oh, dear. That sounded tempting. *Too tempting.*

Liz came back in, oblivious to the unchecked sexual tension flowing between Lily and Gannon. "You were right. Ms. Calder's first available date was June 2, so I tentatively put you all on the schedule." She smiled. "And when I called to confirm with Bode's attorneys, they actually agreed!"

"Despite the wait?" Lily said in shock.

"That's right," Liz confirmed.

"Which means what?" Lily asked warily, aware this seemed a little too good to be true under the circumstances. "They've suddenly decided to be reasonable?"

"Or," Gannon speculated, "given how things went with the visit on Saturday, they've realized they need time for Lucas to get a lot more comfortable with his dad before they go to mediation."

Liz nodded in agreement, adding, "And to that end, they want you to know that Bode intends on seeing Lucas on Wednesday, as per the current visitation schedule."

Once again, Lily had opportunity to regret the unnecessary compromises she had made during the initial custody wrangling, just to get it over with. "So I have to drive Lucas to Dallas?"

"No." Her attorney referred to the notes in front of her. "Bode is coming here to Laramie to have dinner with him. So you may want to prepare Lucas for the fact he will be seeing his dad again. We want this to go as smoothly as possible."

So did Lily. But there was no guaranteeing how her four-year-old would react to the sudden rush of confusing events.

Seeing her uncertainty, Gannon added, "Otherwise, Bode's attorneys will be able to assert you're 'interfering' in the bonding between father and son."

And that, Lily knew, they did not want. "I'll talk to Lucas." Leaving Gannon and Liz behind to tie up a couple of loose ends, Lily headed out.

And received yet another surprise.

A crowd had gathered on the town square to watch competing local news crews report live on the fire statue, while a beaming Harriett Montgomery held court.

FORTUNATELY FOR LILY, the commotion subsided an hour later when the three moving company representatives arrived to give her their estimates of hauling the fire statue to the county fairgrounds.

She expected the bids to be close. Not unanimous!

"Can't do it," the first said.

"Might break," predicted the second.

"No way our insurance carrier will let us take the risk," agreed the third. So Lily called Laramie's premiere independent insurance broker, Greg Savitz, and asked him to meet her on the square and discuss the matter.

"I'm sorry, Mayor," Greg said. "I called all twelve of the carriers I work with and no one will touch the statue. Artwork can be hard to insure in any case, and moving any kind of sculpture is obviously challenging. But this—" Greg gestured to the six-foot-tall smoke-stained ceramic chili pepper "—fire statue could easily crumble if it's jostled, at least so far as anyone can predict. So it's either going to have to stay here—permanently—or you'll have to find another way to move it on your own."

If that were the case, there was only one person Lily could call. Only one person who might be able to talk sense into Harriett Montgomery more easily than her only son. The biggest patron of the arts in the Laramie area and founder of his own Western-themed art museum in his name. Emmett Briscoe.

Luckily for her, the oilman—who'd been at the statue's official unveiling—was still in Laramie County.

Emmett understood her dilemma immediately. "How about I go with you to talk to Harriett?" he asked over the phone.

Lily thought of all she had yet to do before the chili festival commenced on Friday. The dwindling amount of time to accomplish it all. "Could you possibly do it today?" she asked.

GANNON SPENT THE rest of the afternoon drafting the formal response to Bode Daniel's custody motion, and arrived back at the Triple M Ranch just in time to see the surveyors pack up and leave and Lily and Emmett Briscoe arrive. The latter had driven separate vehicles, but it was clear they were there for the same purpose.

It was a little after four o'clock; Lily had been going nonstop all day, and her appearance showed it. Her honey-blond hair had been down around her shoulders earlier, but now it was pulled into a tight, messy knot at the nape of her neck. Her lips were bare, and she looked tired around the eyes, yet her inner determination shone through anyway.

Lily greeted him with a crisp, professional smile that telegraphed none of the affection they'd shown each other over the weekend. As they neared, she extended her hand in greeting, as did Emmett. "Is your mother available?" she asked. "We'd like to talk to her."

Knowing it would take time—and privacy—to woo her, Gannon echoed her cordial tone. "She's in her studio. I'll walk you over."

"So it's true?" Emmett asked. The three of them crossed the newly mown lawn to the converted barn. "You're going to sell to Rex Carter?"

Harriett stepped out to join them. "Over my protestations. Yes, he is."

Feeling as if he was getting a bad rap, Gannon amended, "Not the house or the one hundred acres immediately around it. You will always have a home here, Mom."

She frowned and shook her head. "The view will be obliterated by forty other homes. Your father would be so disappointed to see you let this ranch, which has been in the Montgomery family for generations, go."

Gannon's frustration mounted. "Can we not get into this now?"

"It does seem like a private family matter," Emmett noted gently. The look he gave Harriett reminded them all that Emmett had suffered his own disagreements with his son, Matt, over the dispensation of Briscoe family land. He held out his arm to Harriett. "I would like to see your studio, though. Perhaps you could give me a private tour?"

The two older people exchanged a long, surprisingly in-sync look.

Harriett smiled. "Of course."

Hands on her hips, Lily watched the older couple disappear into the converted barn. "Well, that wasn't how that was supposed to go!"

Glad to be alone with her at long last, Gannon palmed his chest. "You mean you didn't come all the way out here just to see me?"

She warmed at his teasing tone. "I saw you this morning."

"In an official capacity," he corrected.

Lily pivoted, and paced a distance away, her slender hips swaying provocatively beneath her business suit. "I'm here in an official capacity about the statue."

"Why don't you leave that to Emmett? He and my mom have a lot in common." Gannon roamed closer, not stopping until they were only inches apart.

"Such as?" Lily asked softly.

For a moment, he let himself drown in the turquoise depths of her pretty eyes. With a shrug, he ticked off the common ground. "Love of art. Two intractable sons. Spouses now departed that they loved more than life."

Lily inhaled deeply, looking as if she wanted to kiss him again.

And he wouldn't mind if they did. "Give Emmett a little

time to work his magic. Unless—" he paused to study her upturned face "—you have to pick up Lucas?"

She shook her head. "My dad is babysitting him at my house this evening. I was supposed to go with my sister Rose to pick up all the festival posters from the printing company in San Angelo, but she had to leave without me, since I had to take care of this."

"Then you're free for dinner," Gannon guessed, not above taking the opportunity to romance Lily where he found it.

Looking tempted but wary, Lily flushed.

He forged on persuasively before she could refuse. "If you'll help make dinner for the four of us, maybe we can all sit down together," he suggested. "Figure out what to do about the fire statue."

Lily's expression grew even more troubled. "Move it and risk it crumbling—as all the insurance agencies are predicting it might. Or leave it where it sits and endure the constant commotion and complaint."

Gannon realized neither option was good. Especially when the YouTube video making fun of the fire statue was up to a quarter of a million views at last count. His mother had worked long and hard to devote herself full-time to her sculpting and had finally make her mark. She'd made a name for herself all right, but obviously not in the way she wanted. "Exactly why we need a solution ASAP."

Lily peered at him. "Do you have what you need to make a meal on the fly?"

He chuckled and wrapped an arm about her shoulders. "Obviously, you've never seen the Triple M Ranch kitchen."

"Now, THIS," LILY SAID, in glowing respect minutes later, "is what I call a well-stocked larder." A fact that made it all the easier to roll with the latest unexpected turn to her day.

The pantry held every staple imaginable. So did the freezer and fridge. All were neatly organized.

Looking as at home on the ranch as he had been in his loft,

Gannon pulled out a plump roasting hen wrapped in butcher paper. "Beer-can chicken sound good to you?"

Almost as good as another evening spent with you. Lily smiled. "Very."

Gannon took a half dozen spices out of the rack. He measured salt, pepper, paprika, cumin, Mexican oregano and chili powder into the bowl and stirred it into an aromatic mix. "How about I handle that, then, and you do the sides?"

"No problem." Lily selected several yellow squash and two zucchinis, a sweet onion, a bunch of baby carrots and some nice-looking red potatoes. She washed them all, then lined them up on the cutting board. "Should I roast these in the oven or put them on the grill?"

Gannon rubbed the spices into the chicken. "We've got room on the grill."

Lily held the door to the stone patio for him. "How long does it take to roast?"

"An hour and a half." Gannon poured half the beer into a glass, then set the half-full can on the grate, the chicken in a standing position straddling the can. Satisfied, he shut the lid on the gas grill, drank half the remaining beer, then offered her the rest.

It was smooth and mellow, and icy cold. "Nice."

His glance moved over her lazily. "Want another?"

Tingling all over, Lily said, "Sure."

They went back into the kitchen. While Gannon opened up two long-necked bottles of beer, Lily went back to dicing vegetables. She had just tossed them in olive oil and seasoned them with salt and pepper when Harriett and Emmett walked in and announced they were leaving immediately for Fort Worth. "Emmett wants to show me a work in progress at his art museum," Gannon's mother explained with a serene smile.

Unable to help herself, Lily sputtered, "But we were making dinner for everyone!" She had been counting on having chaperones.

Emmett shrugged. "You two go on without us."

That was the problem. Lily feared they would. And not platonically, either.

Oblivious to her worries, Harriett pivoted for the stairs. "I'll just be a minute."

As soon as the three of them were alone, Lily asked Emmett, "Were you able to talk to her about moving her art?"

Emmett shook his head. "Not yet." The oilman took in Lily's worried expression. "Not to worry. I will."

Hearing footsteps on the stairs, he headed for the foyer. The two older people called their goodbyes. A door shut. A motor started. And then…only silence. Lily turned to Gannon, still a little shocked. "What just happened here?" she asked.

Gannon rubbed the underside of his jaw with the flat of his hand. "Hell if I know," he drawled, blue eyes twinkling. "But Emmett seems to have the situation well under control. Maybe I should take a page from his book."

Chapter Eight

Lily caught her breath as Gannon stepped toward her, mischief in his eyes. "What are you doing?"

He grinned. "Picking up where we left off before a dozen other things got in the way." The epitome of masculine confidence, he took her into his arms and tilted her face up to his. "Stating my intentions about where I'd like this relationship to go."

And that was right into dangerous territory. Into a place that carried the promise of unimaginable pleasure and staggering heartbreak.

Afraid if he kissed her again, she really would lose herself in this moment—this man—to disastrous result, Lily spread her hands across his chest. "Listen to me, cowboy," she warned breathlessly, "this is *not* the time to be reckless."

"Good," he chuckled.

Midnight-blue eyes shuttering to half-mast, he vowed in a low, husky voice that further stirred her senses, "Because I'm serious in my pursuit of you."

How long had she waited to hear those very words? Still, Lily moaned in protest. "Gannon…"

He smiled as she said his name. "Lily…" He lowered his lips and kissed her, even more amorously this time.

His chest was so hard and warm, the arms he had wrapped around her so tender, yet strong. Where her breasts pressed against him, she could feel the strong, steady thrumming of his heart beating in harmony to hers. Lower still, there was a tingling need. And then they kissed, over and over again, as if kissing were an end in itself. As if kissing would make everything that had ever held them apart fall away.

Unable to help herself, Lily melted against him and brought him even closer, lifting her lips to his, savoring the hot, dark, masculine taste of him.

Gannon hadn't intended to put the moves on her tonight. He hadn't expected to be alone with her.

But something in the achingly vulnerable way she had looked at him had told him that if he didn't make his romantic intentions clear, here and now, the walls she had been busy erecting around her heart would grow ever higher and ever stronger.

He had missed his chance with Lily once, out of a combination of stubbornness and pride. He wasn't going to miss another. Because he knew now, even if she wouldn't admit it to herself, that the two of them were bound to be together. She filled a void in his life that he hadn't even known existed while slaving away at his job 24/7. And he was pretty sure he made her life better, too.

But she was right about one thing. They did need to slow this down before they hopped into bed again. Make sure that the next time they did make love she would have no regrets.

So slowly, reluctantly, he let the kiss ebb and lifted his head.

He expected Lily to concede his point.

Acknowledge that what they had was something rare and special.

Instead, as she blinked herself into renewed awareness of their surroundings, she looked more strained than ever. Scowling, she unlinked her hands from his neck, put them on his shoulders and gave him a furious shove.

"Once again, you're out of line here, cowboy," she said. Whirling on her heel, she grabbed her bag, then paused to level a lethal look his way. "For both our sakes, make sure it doesn't happen again!"

Giving him no chance to reply, she stormed out.

THE NEXT DAY at noon, Lily looked up from her desk to see her sister Rose walking in. Her triplet sister did a double take at the succulent grilled chicken and roasted vegetables in front of her.

"Since when do you eat anything but fresh fruit and yogurt or cottage cheese for lunch?" Rose teased.

Doing her best to keep her expression inscrutable, even though she was pretty sure everyone in town had heard about Gannon's overture by now, Lily said only, "It was a gift." *From the sexiest cowboy around. The picnic dinner I failed to stick around to enjoy the night before.*

"So I heard." Rose strolled closer. "Have to hand it to Gannon Montgomery." She winked. "That looks really good."

It was, Lily thought, as she finished another bite of tender spiced chicken. Despite everything, she'd been impressed when he'd left the gourmet spread with the town hall receptionist, his thoughtful gesture a direct counterpoint to her rude behavior the evening before. Another of the many things in his favor.

Damn, the man could cook.

And kiss.

And make love…

Lily repressed a groan. She had to stop remembering what it felt like to be in his arms. Otherwise, she really would end up in his bed again.

And if she did…he really would break her heart. Having picked up on her ambivalence, Rose perched on the edge of Lily's desk. "So does this mean you're finally ready to give that cowboy a chance to be your valentine?"

She was.

And she wasn't.

He made her feel so vulnerable—and aroused—and she

hated feeling that way. As if her life were ricocheting out of control. She wanted order and stability, not the temporary mind-numbing pleasure that Gannon had to offer. "We're—" Lily searched for the appropriate word, then finally settled on "—sort of friends. Again."

Rose nabbed a roasted carrot from her plate. "Looks like much more than friendship to me. But then, what do I know—since I've never done anything but strike out in the romance department?"

Nor was the divorced Rose inclined to pursue another relationship. She had her hands full simultaneously running her online local produce business and caring for her two-year-old triplets.

Lily waved off the concern. "He was just showing his appreciation for what I've been trying to do regarding the fire-statue situation."

"How is that going, by the way?"

Lily sighed. She'd spent half the morning on the phone. "I'm still trying to get someone to move it."

"And speaking of men with muscles," Rose remarked wryly, making a suddenly mischievous face.

Lily turned her gaze in the direction of her sister's.

And her heart somersaulted in her chest.

"Hey, Rose," Gannon said, his smirk indicating he'd heard what Rose had said to alert Lily they had company. Sexy male company.

"Hey, Gannon." Rose bounded to her feet. "Well, I'll leave you two alone. Lily, I'll meet you at the loading dock behind town hall in an hour for the poster distribution."

Abruptly, her mind was right back where it should be: on chili festival business. "Did everyone confirm?"

Rose shook her head. "As usual, a few volunteers canceled last minute, but Miss Mim was able to round up a few more to fill in. You still want to do all the rural areas?"

Lily hated to stick that with anyone else, since it was going to be such a long, dull grind. "Yep."

"Okay." Her sister beamed. "See you then." She waved and took off.

Lily turned back to Gannon, determined to be as polite and businesslike as possible today. She had to stop letting him know how much he got under her skin. Because, clearly, it was only encouraging him.

She offered a formal smile. "Thank you for lunch. That was very thoughtful."

"Glad you liked it."

Lily studied his closely shaven jaw, navy corduroy shirt and jeans. He seemed to have had a haircut since the last time she'd seen him, too. "But that's not why you're here." *Looking—and smelling—like you're going on a date, even though it's the middle of the day.*

"Unfortunately, no." Suddenly grim, he studied her, head to toe, his gaze lingering on her eyes. "You haven't heard?"

Lily's heart sank. Judging by the way he was behaving, this had to be bad news. "Obviously not," she admitted, her whole body tensing.

He gestured at her computer. "May I?"

Lily moved away from her desk, catching a drift of sandalwood and soap as he passed. He sat down and quickly did a Google search on Bode Daniels. Immediately, a list of articles came up. He clicked on the one from the Dallas newspaper, filed an hour before.

It's Official, the headlines screamed. Bode Daniels Asked To Step Down as Starting Quarterback for Dallas Gladiators.

Dismayed, Lily continued reading the comments from the team general manager. "We'd like to keep Bode on our roster, as backup QB, of course, but we understand that he may wish to explore his options with other professional organizations as a free agent. And, if so, we wish him well…"

Lily looked at Gannon, so upset about what this meant for all of them that she could barely catch her breath. "So they're really firing him?" she asked.

Gannon nodded. "Pushing him out the door. Paving the

way for keeping him at a greatly reduced salary. Encouraging Bode and his agent to look elsewhere." He leaned back, his big muscular body overwhelming the swivel chair that nearly swallowed her.

Turning toward her, he gestured offhandedly. "Take your pick."

Resisting the urge to sink down on Gannon's lap and take comfort where she could find it, Lily perched on the edge of her desk, facing him. Discreetly she tugged the hem of her skirt to the middle of her knees. "What does this mean for me?"

Gannon stood with an economy of motion. "Maybe nothing."

Lily remained where she was, feeling too shaky to even move back into her desk chair. She tilted her head up to look at Gannon. The compassion in his expression enticed her to articulate her fears. "Or maybe a lot more of a child custody fight than we were bracing for—if Bode remains convinced that his previous lack of interest in Lucas and resultant decline in popularity with the fans is responsible for the loss of his job as starting QB."

A tense silence fell.

Gannon moved to the window overlooking the town square where his mother's charred statue still sat before turning back to Lily. In his casual Western clothing, soft but worn leather jacket and boots, he looked like the down-home rodeo cowboy he had once been, instead of the super successful city lawyer he'd worked hard to become.

She supposed, like her, he was more than just one thing.

He wanted more, too.

She swallowed.

She had to stop thinking about how much alike they were and start focusing on how different. "I gather Liz knows?" she asked finally, wishing she could put all her reservations aside, and simply go to him. Let him take her in his arms and comfort her. Perhaps even kiss…

Gannon sobered even more. "I called her before I came over to tell you."

Lily straightened on trembling legs, appreciating his calm protectiveness. "How'd you find out?"

He ambled toward her. "I set up a news alert for any and all Dallas Gladiators news on my phone," he said.

Lily moved away from her desk, too. "Ah." Smart. And something she couldn't bear to do herself, for fear of what all she might find out.

He caught her before she could pass him. Lightly touched her shoulder, all strong, empathetic male. "You okay?"

Was she?

Lily guessed she was. She had no choice. For her son's sake, she had to be. With effort, she nodded. Gannon looked skeptical.

So Lily flashed a smile and amended her response. "Except for the fact I feel like I was sucker punched in the gut," she conceded with a bitter laugh. "Sure."

One corner of his lips lifted in silent commiseration, and he looked as if he wanted to take her in his arms. She lifted a staying hand.

He let her go instead.

"Speaking of difficult situations... Have you heard from your mom?"

It was Gannon's turn to exhale in frustration. "She's still in Fort Worth with Emmett. They're meeting with some movers who specialize in transporting valuable objects. They hope to have something worked out by tomorrow at the latest."

Lily was glad to hear that. She, too, had come to the conclusion they needed specialized help. "Any idea what that will cost the town?"

"I'm sure it will be expensive, but Emmett Briscoe said he will cover it."

"That's nice of him."

"It is."

Another, more intimate, silence fell.

Lily's desire to throw herself in Gannon's arms grew by leaps and bounds. Forcing herself to ignore her own wants and needs, as well as the tingling in her middle, she glanced at her watch. The poster distribution would start in half an hour. "Well, if that's all…"

Gannon nodded, accepting her brush-off with surprising ease. "I'll let you get back to work."

HALF AN HOUR LATER, Lily found herself on the loading dock behind town hall, squaring off with the beloved Miss Mim, the retired librarian chairing the chili cook-off and festival. "You paired me with someone to distribute the posters and signs?" she asked in amazement. To her knowledge, no one else was working in pairs.

"Yes, dear, I did."

Lily blinked. "Why?"

Miss Mim raised a hand to stop a volunteer from putting the signs in the back of Lily's SUV. "Well, for one thing, it will go faster."

Lily was used to Rex Carter and some of the good old boys hinting she was incapable of carrying out her duties. Not the beloved Miss Mim, who had always supported her. "And another?" she demanded.

Miss Mim smiled mysteriously. "I had a specific request."

This got worse and worse. Lily had been counting on the time alone to sort out her feelings about everything that had happened the past few days. "What about *my* opinion?"

"Well, of course it counts, but why would you resist assistance that will get you done—and back to pick up your son—a whole lot sooner?"

"Maybe because it's me," Gannon drawled, striding up to join them.

Miss Mim scoffed. "Now, why would Lily resist the help of a big strong man, especially one as charming as you?"

She peered at them with a matchmaker's concern. "The two of you aren't still quarreling, are you?"

Gannon winked. "Maybe she's afraid she won't be able to resist me. What with her mind on Valentine's Day and all."

Lily gasped in indignation while everyone within earshot of his audaciousness chuckled.

"Of course..." Ignoring her reddening cheeks, he leaned treacherously close and whispered loudly in her ear, for the benefit of their growing audience, "If you want, Mayor Mc-Cabe, I can unload all fifty of the posters and signs that are already in the back of my pickup truck and move them over to your SUV. Or—" he stood back, propped his big hands on his waist, and surveyed her thoughtfully "—you can do it."

He was right about one thing, Lily realized in exasperation. Time was a'wastin'. Pursing her lips, she accepted the long list of locations from Miss Mim, and then turned back to Gannon. "Let's just go."

"See?" Gannon held up his hands in triumph, beaming at one and all. He settled his Stetson squarely on his head and proclaimed, "I told you she would love the idea once she got used to it."

Once again everyone chuckled.

"It being almost Valentine's Day and all," Gannon added.

Which of course made everyone laugh all the more.

Blushing furiously, Lily marched toward his truck. Although the day had started out sunny, the clouds had rolled in, and the temperature had dipped into the low fifties. She'd thrown on a cashmere wool pea coat to handle the chill, but even she could see it wasn't enough.

Gannon eyed her skirt and heels. "Sure you don't want to change, given where we're headed?"

Lily had intended to stop by her house and do just that before she set out. But the thought of disrobing—with him anywhere in the vicinity—made her change her mind.

Not because of what he would do.

He was, and always had been, a perfect Texas gentleman.

It was herself she was worried about.

The fact he might steal a kiss.

And the knowledge she would certainly react to said kiss kept her from tempting fate in any way, shape or form.

"I'm fine," Lily insisted. She shot him a haughty look before stepping on the running board and swinging herself up into the cab, too late realizing her quick aggressive action had given him more than a flash of her hip and leg.

A flash he sure seemed to be appreciating. "Besides, since you're so big and strong and manly," she purred, settling into the passenger seat and tugging her skirt down as far as it would go, "I expect you'll be doing all the heavy lifting."

He laughed, not the least bit deterred, and climbed in behind the wheel. A few minutes later, they were on their way out of town.

"Seriously, why did you ask to be partnered with me?" Lily asked.

"You seriously have to ask?"

Her mood improving despite herself, she bantered back, "I just did."

"I wanted to spend time with you."

Lily folded her arms in front of her and turned her attention to the passing scenery, which at the moment was mostly wide-open space and sagebrush. "We're not going to end up kissing again," she said.

He remained maddeningly unperturbed. "I didn't expect we would. Today."

Heaven help her. Gannon was indefatigable when he wanted something. And right now that something was clearly her.

Determined to keep their focus on business, she fell silent, speaking only to direct him to the first intersection of country roads on their list, a four-way stop that was widely traveled but rarely held much traffic at any one time, thereby giving a driver and/or passengers ample opportunity to notice the advertisement. He hit his hazard lights and pulled over to the berm.

They got out of the truck. A chill damp wind whipped around them. "Where do you want it?" Gannon lifted the first poster from the bed of the truck.

Lily pointed. "In front of the stop sign."

He obliged her with a smile. "Here?"

"Maybe a little farther back." Lily observed it from several angles, then nodded in approval. "That's good."

The signs for the First Annual Laramie, Texas, Chili Cook-Off & Festival, which had been designed to look like movie posters, were mounted on metal frames that could be pounded several inches into the ground. All featured a man and woman locked in an embrace, with the ruggedly beautiful west Texas landscape behind them. At the top of the sign was the slogan "Put some heat in your Valentine's Day weekend!" The word *heat* had shimmering red-and-gold waves running through it. The bottom of the sign, which listed the dates and times of the festival, ended with the catchy phrase, "Come for the food and the parade, stay late for the music and dancing!"

Gannon shut the tailgate. "I heard it was your idea to give the festival a romantic slant."

Lily nodded, proud of all the hard work that had gone into making this fund-raiser/celebration a success. She walked toward Gannon, not stopping until they stood toe to toe, and said softly, "It made sense to capitalize on the holiday, since couples are always looking for something new and exciting to do on Valentine's Day. But we have other, kid-friendly posters going up, too, advertising the boardwalk-style games and the parade and the pony rides."

Gannon took her hand and gazed intimately into her eyes. "Does this mean you're looking for something fun and romantic to do, too?"

Chapter Nine

Gannon wasn't surprised to see Lily stiffen at his question. "I'll be working on Valentine's Day."

"What if you weren't?" he asked as they drove to the next place on their list, a half mile down the road, and got back out of the truck again.

Lily stalked around to the back and opened the tailgate before he could get there. She had to go up on tiptoe to be able to reach the sign. He didn't mind. It gave him a very nice view of the rounded lower slopes of her derriere, visible beneath her hip-length red cashmere coat.

"I wouldn't celebrate it in any case." Lily huffed in frustration as she tugged the sign toward her, and then, still on tiptoe, lifted it down onto the ground.

Gannon retrieved the rubber mallet—which she couldn't reach—and handed it to her. Lazily, he accompanied her to the intersection. He stood, arms crossed in front of him, while she selected a spot and pounded it in with several hard thwacks.

"Why not?"

Finished, she stalked back to the truck, got another sign and took it to the opposite side of the four-way intersection. Her high heels tapped a decisive staccato over the pavement. Again, he trailed behind, enjoying the view. "Because I don't believe in romance." She thwacked in another sign.

Gannon fell into step beside her as she made her way back to the truck. "What *do* you believe in?"

She climbed back into the truck, the hard rubber mallet still in her hand, and reclasped her safety belt. "The temporary status of relationships."

Gannon moved his gaze away from the tempting softness of her breasts. "What about sex? Do you believe in that?"

Brow furrowing, she studied the next location on their list. "That can be good." She pointed him in the direction she wanted to travel.

"As the two of us recently proved." He made a left turn.

"But it's temporary in nature, too," Lily continued, crossing her legs at the knee.

Gannon stopped at the next intersection on their list. "It's a shame you feel that way."

"Why?"

He cut the motor and turned to look at her. "Because I can't imagine that I would ever stop wanting you."

Lily flushed self-consciously and vaulted out of the truck. She walked along the graveled berm. "What about you?" She lost her balance as her heel caught in a rut. "Do you usually celebrate Valentine's Day?"

Gannon reached out to steady her. "Whenever I'm dating someone, I have." He leaned against the tailgate as the cool winter breeze floated over them. "It's required in any relationship."

Shivering, Lily buttoned up the front of her coat. "But have you wanted to celebrate it?"

Enjoying the moment, just being with her, Gannon shrugged. "In the past? Not really." He let his gaze drift over her, then flashed a persuasive grin. "Now—I'd like to take what's on that poster and magnify it for you a thousand times over."

And if the look on her face were any indication, she wanted that, too. Whether she would ever let them act on it, though, was another question entirely.

"Dɪᴅ ʏᴏᴜ ɢᴇᴛ all finished putting up signs, Mommy?" Lucas asked when she picked him up from school several hours later.

Lily slipped her hand in his. "I did." Together, they walked toward her SUV.

Still a little on edge from events of the previous weekend, he squinted up at her. "Can we have all my favorites for dinner?"

Willing to do whatever it took to reassure him, Lily smiled. She gave him a hug before helping him up into his safety seat. "We sure can."

"Can I play blocks, too?"

"Absolutely." Lily knelt to give him an encouraging hug. She made a playful face. "As long as you build me something really special."

He beamed. "I'll build a ranch!"

Lucas chattered about school during the short drive back to her house. Lily settled him with his toys, then went upstairs to change into jeans and a long-sleeved shirt. She swept her hair up into a clip, and then went back down to the kitchen to start fixing dinner. A couple minutes later the doorbell rang. Somehow, she wasn't surprised to see Gannon standing on the other side.

His expression was all business, and he had a file folder in his hand. "The plans for moving the statue," he explained, his fingers lightly brushing hers as he handed them over. "I thought you might like to see them since waivers are going to have to be signed all around."

Appreciating his efficiency, Lily ushered him in back to the kitchen. She read through the papers quickly. "So they want to move the statue to the fairgrounds, where it will need to be displayed in one of the glass cases in the exhibition buildings, before being moved to Fort Worth?"

Gannon nodded. "As previously discussed, Emmett Briscoe is paying for the moves and the insurance. He's also offering to purchase the statue from the town for the original commission paid to my mother."

Lily paused. "How does Harriett feel about that?"

"Good. Since the town is divided in their opinion regarding the artistic value, she and Emmett both think it might be appreciated more there."

"And they want to do this tomorrow?"

"Everyone figures the sooner, the better."

"Okay." Hearing the water on the stove had started to boil, Lily dumped pasta into the pot. "I'll make the calls now if you want to wait."

Gannon flashed a grin. "I do."

Lucas strolled in. "Hey, Mr. Montgummy."

Gannon hunkered down to shake hands with him, man to man. "Hey there, Lucas."

"Want to play blocks with me?"

Another grin. "I sure do." The two ambled off, hand in hand.

Lily kept an eye on dinner while she talked on the phone. The waiver had to be reviewed by the town attorney, so she sent that to him. She updated the town council members and let them know that an offer had been made to reimburse the town for the statue. It was agreed the matter would be discussed and voted on at the next public meeting. Once the waiver was approved, she called Emmett and Harriett and congratulated them on their quick work, too. Finished, she put down the phone, just in time to see Lucas race back in. "Guess what, Mommy?"

Lily took in her son's happy grin. "What?"

"Mr. Montgummy likes macaroni and cheese, and green beans and applesauce, too! So…can he stay for dinner?"

GANNON HAD NO idea that Lucas was going to put his mom on the spot like that. And yet…something about the way Lily looked, as if she was half hoping he would accept, had him going along with her son's earnest request. "Sounds good to me," he enthused. "I could even take us all out for ice cream after, if you want."

Lucas clapped his hands. "Yesss!"

Lily's eyes gleamed with a combination of exasperation and mischief. "Just so you understand, counselor, Lucas's 'favorite' is the kind of macaroni that comes in a box—with powdered cheese—and canned green beans and store-bought applesauce."

Gannon shrugged, just happy to be included. "Sounds like all the food groups to me."

Lucas clapped his hands, even though Lily was pretty sure her son had no idea what comprised a balanced meal for kids, never mind adults. "It is!" Lucas declared cheerfully.

Gannon looked at her, daring her to retract the invitation. Knowing she wouldn't. Not if it would mean disappointing her young son.

"All right," she said, mimicking their joy. "Give me another twenty minutes to put on the finishing touches…"

"Want to see my toys?" Lucas asked.

"Sure," Gannon smiled.

Lucas took him by the hand and led him over to his toy box. He settled cross-legged on the floor, then waited.

Realizing what was expected, Gannon sat down beside the little boy.

Lucas showed Gannon the ranch he had been building with his blocks. A prairie-style house and barn, surrounded by a fence.

He went back to his toy box. "I've got two horses…" Lucas handed them over.

"Nice." Gannon smiled, unable to help but think how nice it was to spend time with Lily and her son instead of doing what he usually did—work late, and then go home to a take-out dinner and an empty loft. Was this what he had been missing? What it would take to make him feel as content in his home life as Lily and Lucas apparently did in theirs?

"And a longhorn cow." Lucas handed that over, too.

Gannon studied the plastic toy with the reverence it was given, the UT insignia on the mascot's side reminding him of his law school days with Lily. "Very nice." Sentimental, too.

Lucas grinned. He went back to get two cowboys, made to sit astride the saddled plastic horses. "Want to play cowboys on the ranch?"

Gannon nodded.

The two of them assembled the riders and horses, then pretend trotted them around the ranch.

Lily puttered in the kitchen.

And Gannon found himself wishing his time with them would never end.

ALTHOUGH LILY KNEW it would be more than fair to offer Gannon what they were initially planning on eating and nothing more, she also knew a guy his size would not last long on just that. So she threw together a quick salad and took out a couple of chicken breasts. While the guys played with the blocks, she butterflied them, added Southwestern spice and cooked them on her indoor grill.

Gannon's appreciative grin when he saw what was on the table made the extra effort more than worth it.

"How come you're not at work today like my mommy?" Lucas asked, while they were eating.

Gannon dipped a chunk of chicken into barbecue sauce. "You mean back at my office in Fort Worth?"

The tyke nodded, obviously recalling the spacious elegance of the law firm where Gannon worked. "My mommy has to work at her office all the time," Lucas said.

Gannon shot her a curious glance.

Trying not to think how intimate this all suddenly was, Lily speared a bite of salad, then admitted reluctantly, "Since I became mayor, more often than not." She gazed lovingly at her son. "Although on weekends, you go with me a lot of the time, don't you, sweetheart?"

Lucas nodded. "I color pictures and build stuff with my

blocks there. Sometimes we eat stuff from the vending machines at Mommy's desk."

Gannon cast Lucas a fond glance. "Sounds fun."

"So how come you're here and not there?" Lucas asked, still struggling to understand.

Gannon sobered. "Because I have some grown-up things I have to take care of at my family's ranch, and I have to be here in Laramie to do it."

And when he was done, he would be gone again, Lily thought.

Struggling to be positive, she informed Lucas, "Gannon was a cattle rancher and a rodeo cowboy when he was growing up."

The little boy lit up. "Do you have horses?"

Gannon smiled. "We do."

"Do you have cows?"

Gannon frowned. "Not anymore."

Lucas picked up a green bean. "Can I see the horses?"

Lily winced. Given how interested her son was in ranch life versus small town living, she did not know why she had gone down this road. Especially when Lucas was in need of a father figure in his life—and Gannon would be so darn good in the role. If he weren't so career obsessed, that was.

Oblivious to the chaotic thoughts running rampant through her mind, Gannon reached over to give Lucas a friendly pat on the shoulder. "Sure you can."

"When the chili cook-off is over," Lily said, wishing Lucas weren't as enamored with their guest as she secretly was. "If you're still in Laramie," she added cautiously.

If Gannon caught her warning not to lead her son on, he did not show it. "I'll be here another day after the festivities wrap up." He gave her a long, intimate glance. "And maybe, depending on how things go, a number of weekends after that." Smiling broadly, he turned back to Lucas. "In the meantime, if your mother agrees you're old enough, you can ride a pony at the festival."

Lily appreciated the opportunity to veto the notion. "You are," she told her son with a smile.

Lucas turned back to Gannon. "Will you help me?"

Gannon nodded. "I sure will."

"And I'll take the photos," she promised. Conversation fell away as they dug into their food.

"So did you like it?" Lucas said later when they had finished the meal.

"I sure did," Gannon grinned.

He'd certainly eaten like a champ, Lily thought. To the point there were no leftovers—of anything. And her son was clearly enjoying all the undivided attention from his new friend. Of course, in his next breath, Lucas started clamoring for ice cream, and she promised they'd go as soon as the dishes were done. Temporarily appeased, the little boy obediently dashed off to play while Gannon and Lily stayed behind in the kitchen.

"So," Lily teased, after she had put a pot of coffee on for the two of them, "was it really all you hoped?"

"Reminded me of my youth in so many ways. Maybe my future, too."

She nodded at the bowl that had held the mac 'n' cheese. With fresh milk and butter added to the powdered cheese, the pasta wasn't half-bad. But it was still a far cry from the sophisticated adult versions of mac 'n' cheese available these days. She tilted her head, studying him closely. "You really plan to eat that again?" If so, he was full of surprises.

He wrapped his arms around her and brought her close. "I'm sure I will when I have kids. All the time."

Yet another shocker. "So you *do* want a family?" she asked, recalling the earlier conversation they'd had at his loft. He'd been coy with her when she'd broached the subject of settling down, so she'd just assumed he wasn't interested. And, truth be told, she'd always seen him as such a bachelor.

He smoothed the hair from her cheek and admitted softly, "I do."

Lily cast a glance toward the adjacent living area. Lucas was so busy he hadn't seen them yet. But he might. And if he did, he would broadcast the fact they had been—well, not hugging, but not completely innocent of attraction to each other, either.

As if reading her mind, Gannon brushed his thumb across her lip and reluctantly let her go. "What about you?" he asked casually. "Do you want more children?"

Together, they worked to fill the dishwasher as the fragrance of fresh-brewed coffee filled the room. Bumping shoulders, arms and elbows from time to time. Her whole body tingling, Lily shrugged. "Maybe someday if I marry. Otherwise, not."

He watched as she added soap and shut the dishwasher. "Do you plan to marry?"

A soft whirring noise filled the kitchen as the machine started. She poured two cups of coffee and got out the cream and sugar. "I'm not counting on it, but I'm not ruling it out, either."

He moved toward her. "What would make you say yes?"

Being irrevocably in love with someone—like you, Lily thought. Unwilling to let herself be that vulnerable, however, she simply said, "Being with someone who could meet me halfway."

His tender smile affected her like the softest caress. "Ah, a compromiser."

Lily studied him over the rim of her mug. "And you're still not."

The smile on his lips reached his eyes. "Not when it comes to anything vitally important," he acknowledged quietly. "And for good reason. Too much compromise is what nearly ruined both my parents' lives."

Lily blinked. "How so?" she asked, aware it wasn't like Gannon to reveal such sensitive information. Especially when it came to his private family life.

Gannon took a seat at the kitchen island, prompting her

to do the same. He propped one elbow on the counter and turned toward her, his knees nearly grazing hers. "My dad wanted to be an electrical engineer, but his dad pressured him into staying on the ranch, as tradition warranted. So he did—but his heart wasn't in it, and he was never very good at it." Remorse colored his low tone.

Shrugging, Gannon held her gaze and forged on, "As a consequence, my dad seemed to get the short end of every business deal, and the ranch was barely in the black." He grimaced. "If it hadn't been for my mom's salary and the benefits she brought in from the school district, we probably would have had to sell the land."

No wonder he worked so hard to prove himself, Lily thought.

"And you know my mom's story." He took a deep draught of coffee.

Lily stirred cream into her own mug. "She always wanted to sculpt."

"But until she retired, there was no time or money for such an endeavor." His expression darkened. "The bottom line is, neither of my parents were very happy in their work growing up. Even as a kid, I saw that. And I vowed I would never let the same happen to me."

Lily sipped. "*Are* you happy as a lawyer?"

Gannon helped himself to more coffee. "There are ups and downs, but overall, yeah, there's nothing I would rather do."

"I envy your conviction."

He covered her hand with his, his fingers infusing hers with warmth. Lily looked down at their clasped hands, and couldn't help but remember how nice it had been when they had made love. How much she wished she could put all her fears aside and risk it all again.

But common sense told her not to put her heart on the line, even as she lifted her gaze to his once more.

He studied her, with the same burning need to understand. "You don't feel the same career satisfaction?"

Lily shook her head, admitting what she hadn't even told her family. "I never have—about anything except being a mom." That, she loved with a ferocity that still surprised her.

"I'm done!" Lucas called.

Together, they went in to see his creation. It was, in short, amazing. He had torn down his original creation and built something much grander. The architecture blocks formed a rectangular fort, with a two-story house on one end, a barn and several corrals another. He had put all his ranchers inside the central courtyard. Horses in one corral. Cattle in another. "See what a big ranch I have?" he said.

Gannon grinned. "Your cowboys and cattle and horses are very well protected."

Lily hugged her son. "I love it, too."

Delighted he had been able to impress them both, Lucas beamed. "Can we get ice cream now?"

"You bet," Lily and Gannon said in unison.

It had grown dark, so they decided to drive the short distance to downtown. It was also a little chilly, so they elected to sit at a table inside the Dairy Barn to enjoy their treats.

A mistake, Lily noted, since two of her sisters, her triplet Violet—on a break from her medical residency—and the oldest of all the McCabe daughters, Poppy, an interior designer, were there, too.

They immediately ambled over, burgers and milk shakes in hand.

"Fancy finding you here," Violet said.

"We already ate our dinner," Lucas announced proudly. "So Mr. Montgummy said we could go get ice cream."

Violet gave Lily a teasing look. "You cooked for him?"

"Not that the way to a man's heart is through his stomach or anything," Poppy added with her usual dry humor.

"Actually, I think it might be the other way around," Gannon put in. "Since I've cooked for Lily more than she's cooked for me."

Violet and Poppy nodded. "Ah, yes, we heard about the

lunch that got delivered to town hall earlier today. Rose said it looked amazing."

Mischief crinkled the corners of Gannon's eyes. "Maybe I should have all you McCabe ladies out to my place."

Lily groaned and buried her face in her hands. "You don't want to do that."

"Why not?" Lucas asked.

Gannon looked as if he wanted to know, too.

"You have no idea what it's like to be around that much estrogen," Lily explained.

Violet sized him up. "Oh, I think he could handle it."

Maybe so. "But I couldn't," Lily said firmly.

And, as far as she was concerned, that was that.

"So HOW COME you don't want your sisters to know about us?" Gannon asked when Lucas went off to play a quick game of pinball with his "ants" before they left the Dairy Barn.

"Because there's nothing to tell."

His eyes darkened emotionally, and her throat suddenly went dry. Lily tried again. "Because they'll tell my folks."

"And you really don't want them to know."

Lily scraped her spoon across the bottom of her sundae cup, embarrassed to have to admit, "My parents were upset enough about my liaison with Bode when that happened, never mind the aftermath. They live in fear I'll make another mistake, this time one that will impact not just me, but my son."

His knees pressed against hers under the table, forcing her to look up. "Your parents live in fear?" he asked bluntly. "Or you do?"

Good question, Lily thought, moving back so their knees were no longer touching. And one she really did not want to contemplate.

Fortunately, she didn't have to discuss it further, because at that moment, her two sisters returned with a very weary-looking Lucas between them. By the time she and Gannon made the short drive back to her bungalow, Lucas was sound asleep.

"Want me to carry him in for you?" Gannon offered.

Although Lily could still do it when necessary, Lucas was pretty heavy for her now. And she was dead tired. "If you wouldn't mind." Lily undid the straps and helped ease her son from the seat. Gannon carried him upstairs to his toddler-size bed.

Knowing sleep was more vital than pajamas at that point, Lily eased off Lucas's socks and shoes, tucked his Blue Blankie and stuffed horse in beside him. She covered him, turned the night-light on and eased from the room. By the time she had tiptoed down to the first floor, Gannon was waiting for her in the hall, looking handsome and expectant. He flashed a sexy smile, then drawled, "I don't suppose you're going to ask me to stay?"

Lily shook her head. She was way too vulnerable where he was concerned. "Not tonight."

"All right, then." He swept her into his arms and bent her backward from the waist. Ignoring her gasp of dismay, he gave her a smoldering look and then lowered his head to hers. "I guess this will have to hold us over until the next time you do ask me to stay."

Lily barely had time to suck in a breath, and then his lips were on hers in a devastatingly slow kiss that rocked her world.

When he finally let the sensual caress come to a halt and righted her slowly, she was dizzy and tingling all over, wanting more. So much more, damn that ornery man!

He grinned, as if he knew exactly how she was feeling. "Good night, Lily." He kissed her temple and walked out the door.

Chapter Ten

Lily stared at Miss Mim and the other members of the steering committee for the chili cook-off late Wednesday morning, sure she couldn't have heard right. Outside, the movers were busy first securing, then moving the ceramic chili pepper statue off the town square.

"The governor and his wife are coming to the festival?" What had started out to be a mostly local fund-raiser was quickly turning into an event beyond their wildest dreams.

"Not for the entire thing, of course. But they'll be here on Saturday in time for the judging. They'll sample the winning entrees and leave after the first dance."

Aware she was way too distracted, Lily moved away from the windows and the sight of Gannon, Harriett Montgomery and Emmett Briscoe, who were overseeing the delicate procedure.

"Rex Carter pulled it off," Marybeth Simmons, the PTA president, said.

"I'm impressed," Lily said to the former mayor.

He accepted her compliment with a nod. "We're still way short on important dignitaries, but I'm working on reeling a few more in to give us the kind of visibility we need to really put Laramie on the map."

"Good to hear," she said sincerely. "I also hear congratulations are in order to you for the sale of the Triple M."

"It's not definite yet."

"But it will be," Lily ascertained.

For the first time in recent memory, Rex Carter looked less than absolutely confident. "When I get Gannon Montgomery to sign off on it, then, yes, it will be," he said.

Frowning, Miss Mim added her two cents. "Harriett doesn't want to sell. Although, since her late husband left the majority of the land to her son and the house to her, she doesn't have much say in the matter."

"It's time," Rex said confidently.

Without warning, Lily's assistant charged in. "I'm sorry to interrupt, but Liz Cartwright-Anderson—your attorney—said you have to turn on the television right now! Channel 11!"

Lily walked to the TV in the corner. Quickly switched it on.

The screen was filled with breaking news. Front and center was Bode Daniels, standing behind a bank of microphones. He was flanked by Viviana on one side, his agent on the other. "First of all," Bode was saying with utter sincerity as he looked directly into the camera, "I want to thank the team for the opportunity they've given me, and to the fans for all the support over the years."

"Bode!" A reporter attending the press conference shouted. "What's your reaction to the news the Gladiators are ready to cut you loose?"

Oh, no, Lily thought, really fearing what that could mean for her and her son. Especially if her ex's search for a new team got desperate, as some seemed to think it might.

Bode flashed his trademark grin. Shrugged. "I wouldn't get too worked up about what is essentially a contract negotiation at this point."

The reporters all chuckled at his deadpan humor.

"Would you consider going elsewhere to play?"

"I'm a Texan, born and bred, so of course I'd like to stay in the Lone Star State for the remainder of my pro career."

"So since you obviously haven't forgotten your small-town

Texas roots, would you stay here in Dallas for less money?" someone shouted.

Bode sobered. "I don't think anyone wants to feel like they're moving backward. Especially when you're still at the height of your abilities."

"Does that mean you're not willing to take second place?"

"I did that, early in my career," Bode declared. "So, no, I have little interest in going down that road again."

"There are reports that your inability to see your young son, Lucas, has proved to be a distraction this past season. Is that true?"

Inability! Lily fumed. Since when had Bode been *unable* to see his son? More like *uninterested* and *unwilling*!

Another flash of that megawatt smile. "You're right, Chet." Bode addressed the reporter by name. "I haven't seen enough of my son. But I'm working on remedying that. And in fact—" he winked "—I'm on my way to Laramie, Texas, to see him right now. So if you all will excuse me…" Commotion reigned on screen as the press conference abruptly broke up.

Lily switched off the TV.

Miss Mim looked at Lily, clearly concerned. "Did you know Bode was coming to town?"

She nodded, her heart sinking. "He's having dinner with Lucas this evening." And now everyone else who had been watching that press conference or would catch it later on the internet would know it, too.

BY FOUR O'CLOCK, word had spread. Reporters and film crews from all over the state had started showing up, along with a few paparazzi who mostly covered professional sports figures.

At four-thirty, Lily received a text from Bode, telling her where and when he wanted her to drop her son off.

Luckily for Lily, Gannon had once again made himself available. And this time she had not argued in the slightest.

Maybe it was wimpy of her, but she wanted him by her side. And not just for legal backup—while Liz handled the client appointments and court appearances she had already set up for that day—but for emotional support, too.

"You okay?" Gannon asked quietly.

Lily nodded. *Now that you're here with me, I am.* Resisting her desire to throw herself into Gannon's strong arms, she murmured, "This morning, before I dropped him off at school, I talked to Lucas about the fact he was probably going to be seeing his dad tonight."

His brow furrowed in concern, Gannon prodded, "And...?"

She swallowed. "He seemed okay about it—since he didn't have to go to his dad's place again."

Gannon met her eyes, soothing her as only he could. "He'll be in familiar surroundings."

Lily nodded.

About that, she was very grateful. As for the rest...not so much.

Because it was an unseasonably warm February day, Bode had bought out the putt-putt golf course for the rest of the day. And asked the local restaurant, Sonny's Barbecue, to cater a party for thirty.

Thirty!

Lily turned to Gannon as soon as she'd heard the news. "Is it me, or does that seem excessive to you, too?" As if her ex really did not know how to interact with anyone one-on-one these days.

Gannon shook his head. "Maybe he just likes having an entourage along."

Lily sighed. "The next question is, who is in the group?"

They found out when she and Gannon picked up Lucas at school and drove him over to the miniature-golf course.

To her surprise, instead of just his usual team of public relations experts and lawyers, Bode had his entire immediate family there, including his parents, his grandparents, his brother and sister and their kids.

Lily had never met any of the extended Daniels clan. Nor, of course, had her son or Gannon.

They all met them now.

"So THESE ARE all your cousins," Bode concluded to Lucas, waving at two little girls and three boys, all of whom were roughly close to Lucas's age. "Would you like to play putt-putt with us?"

Lucas turned to look up at Lily.

Determined to be as calm and courteous as the situation required—if it killed her—Lily smiled at her son encouragingly. "It looks fun!"

Lucas wavered, uncertain. He looked at Gannon.

"To me, too," Gannon said cheerfully.

Lower lip sliding out into a nervous pout, he looked up at Lily and Gannon beseechingly. "Are you going to play, too?"

Lily could tell Bode wanted and needed to handle this on his own this time. A glance at Gannon seemed to indicate he had observed the same.

Mindful of the press, who were held back to the other side of the street by sheriff deputies dispatched to handle the crowd, Lily knelt down to her son. At just over sixty degrees, it was slightly chilly and likely to get more so as the sun went down; she zipped up his fleece-lined hoodie. She was about to reach into her purse for his hat when Bode beat her to the punch and produced a knit Gladiators cap for their son to wear.

Lily suppressed a sigh.

Of course. She should have known Bode and his PR team would not resist any opportunity to pull at the public's heart-strings. Cognizant that Lucas was looking at her curiously, able to feel Gannon's wordless support, she put her personal feelings aside and slipped on the cap that would keep Lucas warm.

Smiling, she informed him, "I've got some more stuff to

do for the chili cook-off while you have dinner here tonight with your daddy and the rest of your cousins."

Cousins being the magic word.

There was nothing Lucas liked more than playing with cousins. She ran her hands lovingly over his small shoulders and looked straight into his eyes, transferring every bit of confidence she possessed, so that he, too, would feel the same.

"But Gannon and I will be back before bedtime to get you," she finished softly. "Does that sound okay?"

Lucas nodded. Experience had taught him he could count on her always. And he was fast learning that he could count on Gannon, too.

Lily rose, pretending for all their sakes that she was dropping him off just as she did every day at school. "Okay, then, I'll see you later." She hugged her son to her one last time and somehow managed to speak around the ache in her throat. "Now go play."

"Okay, Mommy." Reassured, Lucas smiled and waved. Bode took Lucas's hand as cameras flashed. Together, Daddy and son headed off to join the cousins—while Lily walked off, successfully fighting tears, Gannon at her side.

"Where now?" Gannon asked her as soon as they were out of earshot. Because they both knew they were also under scrutiny, they walked a discreet distance apart.

"My house." Lily turned and gave Gannon a casual smile.

That quickly, a flash went off.

Reminded once again what it was like to live under the harsh glare of the limelight, Lily added, "As soon as I talk to my cousin, Kyle." A deputy with the sheriff's department, he had been dispatched to work the crowd.

"Hey." She hugged the big, brawny lawman hello.

"You don't have to ask," Kyle said kindly before she could speak. He shook hands with Gannon, too. "Of course I'll keep an eye on Lucas for you."

Lily exhaled in relief. "You'll let me know if he seems the least bit upset?"

The deputy nodded. Like the rest of the McCabes, Kyle was not just protective of those around him, but also very loving and supportive. "Where are you going to be?"

"My house." Or in other words, just a few blocks away, on Spring Street. "I'll have my cell with me at all times."

"Consider it done, then."

Lily saw some reporters headed toward her. Gannon and Kyle exchanged glances. Gannon moved Lily off to the side while Kyle amiably blocked any pursuit of her.

It wasn't hard. The reporters could always go after Lily later; it was Bode and his son they wanted access to now.

Once at her house, Lily set her purse down. Closed the blinds. Kicked off her shoes. Then stood, not sure what to do or where to go next. And that was when the tears finally started to fall.

GANNON HAD BEEN expecting the storm. He was glad he was there to comfort her. "Hey, hey, now," he murmured, pulling her close.

Lily buried her head in his shirt, her tears flowing fast and thick. "Can't help it."

It broke his heart to see Lily so upset, but he loved the feel of her pressed up against him. Gannon stroked a hand down her spine. "He's going to be okay."

"I know that." Lily moved back far enough so that they could look into each other's eyes. She grabbed a handful of tissues from the box on the table and blotted her face. "It's me I'm worried about." She shook her head anxiously and paced over to throw the damp tissues away.

She whirled to face him, her expression even more vulnerable. "What if Bode decides he really does want Lucas in his life?" She drew a quavering breath. "All this time I've gotten used to having him all to myself. I never had to worry about not having my little boy with me on holidays or week-ends because Bode didn't want him. Now…"

Lily's voice caught. "Damn it all, Gannon!" Resentment glittered in her eyes. "Bode bought out the entire putt-putt golf course for the evening. I'm not an heiress! I can't compete with that!"

Tenderness welling from deep inside him, Gannon pulled her back into his arms and ran a thumb over the curve of her cheek. "And you don't have to," he said softly.

Snuggling closer, she said in a low, muffled voice, "You say that now…"

He pressed a kiss to her temple, aware she was struggling not to cry again. "I will always say that." He tightened his arms around her protectively and looked deep into her eyes. "You're incredible, Lily. Lucas knows that. And heaven knows, I see that, too."

She shifted so she could gaze into his eyes. She stared at him a long careful moment while he tried to figure out what to do or say to make her feel better.

Her lips parted. She rose on tiptoe. And then he knew. He was what she wanted. And she was what he wanted, too.

He lowered his head, intending just to kiss her. Knowing if they got started, they might not be able to stop. The hell of it was, he didn't want to stop. And given the way she was pressed up against him, her mouth fused hotly with his, Lily did not want to call a halt, either. Which made their coming together this way all the sweeter.

Her body was soft and warm as it molded to his. Her lips acquiescent one minute, then were feisty as all get-out the next.

He could feel her fighting her desire, just as he was. And he could feel her losing the battle, just as she had the first time they made love.

Not wanting her to regret this the way she had their first, he groaned. Then lifted his head. "Lily…"

She caught the nape of his neck in her hand and pulled him

back. "No talking!" She kissed him again, one hand fisted in his hair, the other sweeping down his body, the softness of her breasts abrading the hardness of his chest. He reacted in kind, letting his hands travel over the delectable curve of her buttocks, her hips, the insides of her thighs. She moaned as he pulled up the hem of her skirt and caressed her through her tights, then pushed her back against the wall, positioning his thigh between hers. She moaned again, a helpless little sound that sent his senses reeling. One hand reaching for his fly, she deepened the kiss even more, her mouth pliant beneath his, her body soft, supple, surrendering.

He unbuttoned her blouse, parted the edges, teased the straps of her bra down her arms. Peeling away the satin, he revealed the upper slopes of her breasts and the taut pink nipples. He kissed her again, hotly, fiercely. His spread fingers tantalized the pebble-hard tips of her breasts, while lower still, he found his way beneath her clothes to the hot, wet silk of her, exploring, stroking, until she moved her hips, rubbing against him, into him, and he was shuddering with need himself.

And still he put everything he had into the kiss, determined that this time would be every bit as memorable as she deserved, so memorable she would not be able to walk away...

Lily groaned softly, impatient as always, her body shivering with need. "Too slow..." With a mewl of frustration, she finally found her way into his pants and reached out to claim him with her hand.

Her tender caress was enough to almost send him over the edge.

Lower still, her thighs parted. "Now, Gannon, now."

Driven by the same frantic need, he stripped off her tights and panties. She helped him dispense with jeans and boxers. He caught her by the hips, lifting her right where she needed to be, her spine pressed against the wall, her arms wound around his shoulders, her legs wrapped around his waist.

Ignoring her raspy intake of breath, he looked into her eyes and kissed her again. "Tell me what you want…"

"You."

He possessed her an inch at a time, with a slowness that was as tantalizing to him as it was to her.

"Tell me what you need…"

She closed tight around him. "You," she whispered again.

He plunged and withdrew, and plunged again. Until her heart was beating in urgent rhythm with his. Until he was aware of every soft inch of her, inside and out.

He hadn't known his control could be so easily lost, but it was.

He hadn't known he could want and need like this, but he did.

And then the last of his reason fled.

She was pressed so intimately against him, he was buried so deep in her, their kisses so rough and heartfelt, he no longer knew where her body ended and his began. They were free-falling into a sweet oblivion that had always been, and always would be, their destiny.

LILY COLLAPSED AGAINST Gannon, her body thrumming with the kind of intimate satisfaction she had never even dreamed existed.

Prior to this, she'd thought she had known what it was to enjoy the physical side of a relationship.

The truth was, she hadn't a clue.

When Gannon made love to her, something unexpectedly wanton was unleashed inside her, to the point all restraint fled. He made her feel cherished and adored, as if nothing else mattered but the two of them and what they felt now.

He tore the walls around her heart away, and she knew if they made love again, she would risk falling in love with him. And that wasn't good. Now, more than ever, with everything she had going on, she needed to keep a tight rein on her emotions. Her happiness—and her son's—depended on it.

With a soft exhalation of breath, she untangled her body from the hard length of his and moved away. While he watched her in lazy satisfaction, she gave up trying to dress and wrapped herself in a throw. Her back to him, she sat down and said, with every ounce of willpower she possessed, "I can't keep doing this—to make myself feel better."

She heard a rustling of clothing behind her. When he sat down across from her, he'd already pulled on his jeans. He also looked a heck of a lot more accepting, and ready for whatever came next, than she felt.

He took her hands in his, his midnight-blue eyes sparkling with mischief. "What better reason to make love?"

Maybe the act of actually being in love?

Embarrassed, Lily extricated her hands from his and, once again, moved away. Feeling as if this was an argument she would never win—especially with her whole body still shimmering with the afterglow of their passion—she went to her purse and pulled out her phone. To her relief, her cousin picked up on the first ring.

"Deputy McCabe."

"Kyle." Trying not to feel so disheveled, Lily shoved the hair from her face. She paced even farther from the chair where Gannon lounged. Ignoring how delectably mussed he looked, she forced herself to concentrate on the larger problem at hand. Bode—and her son.

"How is everything?" she asked, surprised how normal her tone could sound when in reality her entire world had been turned upside down.

While she listened, Kyle relayed in great detail what had happened thus far.

"That's good to hear," Lily said finally. "I'll pick him up at nine o'clock." Which was way past her son's normal bedtime. "Yes, I'll see you then." She ended the call, not sure whether she was more irked about the whole ordeal or relieved that her son was fine.

Gannon looked at her expectantly. She set her phone on

the coffee table and sank down on the sofa, catty-corner from him. "Lucas seems to be having the time of his life with his cousins. Of course, the film crews are having a field day with all the footage."

Gannon considered the implications. "Maybe that'll help Bode get what he wants."

"Yeah, well, what will help *me*?" Lily shot back before she could stop herself.

Gannon grinned and reached for her, as if he had just the answer.

She gasped as he hauled her onto his lap, and her make-shift cover came partially undone.

He pushed the edges of the soft throw aside even more. Her breath caught as his fingers skimmed the insides of her bare thighs. "Gannon…"

He tugged it all the way off and gathered her closer still. Pressing kisses in her hair, along the top of her ear, the nape of her neck, he growled playfully, "That's Mr. Montgummy to you."

She released a shaky laugh despite herself. Not sure whether she wanted to make love with him again, or run away, or both. All she knew for certain was that he made her feel vulnerable. He made her feel…loved. Aware what a ridiculously crazy notion that was, she tried to fight against it. But when he continued to look at her with all the tenderness she could have ever wished for, she could feel her heart opening all the more. "You're going to make me cry."

"Well, we can't have that," Gannon told her gruffly.

And then he made love to her all over again.

THE HOUSE PHONE rang as Lily stepped out of the shower.

It was still only eight o'clock, but she had insisted she and Gannon call a halt to any further amorous activity, just in case Lucas had another meltdown or decided he wanted to come home early.

Hurriedly, she wrapped herself in a robe and rushed

downstairs. Gannon was already headed her way. "Did you get that?"

Gannon nodded. "It was Liz. She wants us to check the message boards for the Gladiators website. She said they're going crazy."

Lily turned on her computer. Together, they scrolled through the team's site.

Lily blinked in surprise. "For every fan who feels sorry for Bode, there seem to be two or three who think he's a dead-beat dad—at least when it comes to spending time with his son." Her spirits lifted. "Maybe this won't work out so well for him after all, then."

Gannon grinned. "Could be, justice will prevail…"

Lily hoped so. In any case, they would soon find out.

"I GOT TO sit on Daddy's lap and talk to the reporter" was the first thing Lucas said to Lily and Gannon once all his good-byes and thank-yous were said.

Lily looked at Gannon, relieved to find she wasn't the only one concerned. Doing her best to hide her inward tension, she put her son in her SUV. "During the putt-putt game?"

"No." Lucas yawned and smiled at Gannon. "While we were eating our dinner. The reporter lady said I was cute. So did the PB&J lady."

It took a moment for Lily to decipher that. "The PR lady?"

"That's what I said." Lucas beamed proudly. "She said the football fans were just going to *go crazy* over me and my daddy. An' it was gonna turn the whole thing around…" Lucas's small body sagged as he rubbed his eyes. "But that's not even the best part. Mr. Cartoon…"

Lily paused to decipher the mangled name. Finally, she guessed, "Mr. Carter?" It made sense Rex would show up at something like that. "The man who used to be the mayor of Laramie?"

Lucas nodded. "He said that my daddy was going to come back to Laramie and eat the best chili and be a great big star of the festival, too! And Daddy said no problem, he would talk about it on TV."

Of course, Lily thought. It wouldn't have been Bode if there hadn't been some sort of self-serving, aggrandizing publicity involved.

Chapter Eleven

Lily called Rex Carter as soon as she got Lucas to sleep. To no avail. The former mayor wasn't answering.

Meanwhile, Gannon, who had rolled up his sleeves and loosened another button on his shirt, used her desktop computer to do his own research.

"Okay, it looks as though Bode taped an interview with ESPN—to be aired this weekend—and another with a local Dallas TV station that's airing tonight on the ten o'clock news."

It was a little stuffy downstairs, so Lily opened two windows in the family room. Cool evening air floated in, giving immediate relief.

"I can't see it on TV—since we don't get that channel on our cable—but we can watch it on the web." She pulled up a chair.

Gannon scooted over slightly to make room for her. Still feeling warm, she took off her cardigan, or tried—one of the sleeves was stuck to her blouse. Gannon helped her.

Lily flushed, aware the last time he'd helped her remove an article of her clothing, they had ended up in bed, making love.

But this time, he was a perfect gentleman.

They waited anxiously through the breaking news headlines. A six-car crash on the Central Expressway. A school board vote. And finally, the third big story of the day. Bode Daniels.

First, they showed the Gladiators' formal announcement regarding Bode's future being read to the press by the current general manager of the team. Then Bode's own comments in his abbreviated press conference that very morning.

"Fortunately," the pretty sports reporter continued, "KJTW was able to get an exclusive interview with the renowned quarterback." They cut to the tape. The same reporter appeared, asking questions. At first, the shoot was in the den of Bode's Dallas home, where he sat surrounded by all his trophies, Gladiators paraphernalia and team photos. His wife was next to him. Smiling, too.

Toni Foley, the reporter, crossed her legs and leaned toward Bode urgently. "It's public record that your future with the Gladiators is up in the air. But what do you say to those who blame you for the team's losing season?"

With Viviana cheering him on wordlessly, Bode turned and looked straight into the camera. "I accept full responsibility for the Gladiators not making the play-offs last season. A team can only go so far without their QB being at the very top of his game. I wasn't." Bode paused, his expression fierce. "If contract negotiations go as I hope and I stick around next season, I will be a force to be reckoned with. I can promise you that. I don't accept failure, and neither should anyone else who roots for me."

Toni ruffled through the papers on her lap. "Some are saying your personal life is to blame here, too. Specifically, your estrangement from your four-year-old son with Laramie, Texas, mayor Lily McCabe."

Lily moaned. "I wish they hadn't mentioned that." Now the town hall would be getting calls about that, too.

"Some are even questioning why Lucas does not carry your last name, but instead goes by the surname of McCabe." Toni looked perplexed. "Was that your choice?"

"More like Viviana's," Lily fumed, as Bode reached over and clasped the supermodel's hand. "She didn't want any children but hers carrying Bode's last name."

On the monitor, Bode paused, clearly considering how to answer that. "I was never okay with that. But—" he straightened in his chair and pushed on "—it was what Lucas's mother wanted, and it had already gotten so ugly between us…" He paused, shook his head, playing the total victim now.

"Only because you refused to admit paternity and publically accused me of lying about it!" Lily wadded up a piece of paper and threw it at the computer screen.

Bode continued with a rueful shrug, as if asking for forgiveness. "I didn't want to fight her on anything else at that point."

"So the rumors are true? The two of you *are* in an ongoing custody battle for your son?"

Bode didn't answer. But it was clear the answer to that was yes.

Lily groaned again.

Onscreen, Toni rushed on. "Is this what was distracting you last season? An inability to even see your only son?"

Bode glanced away a long moment.

"His PR team is probably mouthing the answers he should be giving," Lily said, fuming.

"Probably," Gannon agreed. He draped a protective arm around her shoulders and squeezed.

Finally, Bode looked back at the camera, with a mixture of feigned sadness and determination. "It's a terrible thing when a father can't see his son, but my lawyers and I are working to remedy that. And in fact, you're welcome to tag along with us, Toni, to meet the little tyke, if you like…"

The next shots were taken at the putt-putt golf course in Laramie. Bode swinging Lucas up in his arms for a playful hug. Then later, sitting at one of the picnic tables, enjoying the local barbecue.

"Lucas," Toni said, as the cameras moved in close. "Is this your daddy?"

Lucas basked in the attention. "Yes, it is!" Then he held

up a toy Gladiators football for the reporter to see. "And he's a quarterboy, too!"

Everyone laughed, as Bode corrected playfully, "Quarterback…"

"One more thing," Toni said, reacting to a piece of paper just given her. "The word is you'll be back in Laramie on Friday to be the grand marshal of the parade and head judge for the First Annual Laramie, Texas, Chili Cook-Off and Festival on Friday."

"Wait a minute," Lily cried, suddenly understanding what her son had tried to tell her. She turned to Gannon. "You're the head judge and grand marshal!"

Gannon shook his head, seemingly impressed by all the machinations, despite himself. "Apparently, not anymore…"

Toni continued reading from the paper in front of her, "It's a two-day event over Valentine's Day weekend, folks, so if you want to see Bode in person and throw him your support, that would be a great time to do it!"

Bode looked straight into the camera and turned on his megawatt charm. "I hear there's going to be dancing and music both nights. The food is going to be outstanding. And all proceeds go to the local charities. So my son and I hope to see you all there!"

The film cut.

"So there you have it," Toni concluded with a satisfied smile over her exclusive interview. "Though whether or not Bode Daniels will remain with the Gladiators is yet to be seen…"

The story over, the newscast moved to the next piece.

Lily leaped to her feet. "I can't believe any of that!" She shoved her hands through her hair, not sure whether to scream or cry, just knowing she wanted to do both. "Bode lied about me! Then he used Lucas to evoke sympathy for his plight."

Nodding grimly, Gannon sat back in his chair and folded

his arms across his broad chest. "And trampled all over you and your reputation in the process."

Yet again, Lily thought. She looked at Gannon, knowing she had never felt this miserable. "He really is a bastard, isn't he?" she whispered, pressing a trembling hand to her lips. "I mean, you were right when you told me I shouldn't go out with him even once."

Gannon rose and took her in his arms. He smoothed a hand down her back and held her close, pressing a kiss into her hair. "I might have had an ulterior motive there," he confessed.

Lily drew back to see into his face. "What?"

He brushed a thumb across her cheek, the brooding look back in his eyes. "The fact I didn't want you dating anyone but me."

Lily extricated herself and stepped back. "But you had stopped asking me to go out with you by then! Stopped even wanting to be my friend, really."

"I've never liked tilting at windmills." With an impatient sigh, he continued, "Thinking I'd ever have any kind of future with you back then seemed like just that."

Lily had barely had time to absorb that confession when her house phone rang. She rushed to get it before it could wake Lucas. It was Liz Cartwright-Anderson. Then her parents called—on her cell—which had a much softer ringer. Followed by all five of her sisters and a couple of her cousins, as well as friends.

Finally, Lily recorded a new message on her machine that said she was fine, she wasn't alone and she would talk with everyone tomorrow.

And she realized, in amazement, turning off the ringer on her phone, she *was* fine. Mostly because Gannon was with her.

She hadn't yet had a chance to catch him up on the latest. "Liz wants to meet at her office, after I drop Lucas off at school tomorrow, to craft a strategy to respond. I'm going to invite my immediate family." She paused, not sure how he would feel about this. "I'd like you to come, too."

He looked down at her, all calm, implacable male. "As a legal consultant to Liz?" he asked huskily.

A shiver of need swept through her. She took his hand in hers, clasped it warmly. "That, and my friend."

Smiling with satisfaction, he wrapped his arm about her waist and drew her close. "Well, from one *friend* to the other, I don't think you should be alone tonight," he murmured.

"Don't worry...I won't be."

"Oh, really?" he asked tenderly. "Who's spending the night with you?"

Lily took another gigantic leap of faith. She looked deep into his eyes. "You. I hope. Although it will have to be on the couch, since Lucas might wake up, and I wouldn't want him to think..."

Gannon hugged her close, and then gently kissed her temple and the top of her head. "I understand," he whispered against her ear. "And I'd be happy to stay."

For a moment, Lily luxuriated in the feel of the strong arms around her and the steady thrumming of his heart. It was a new experience, leaning on a man for support. She was surprised by how much she liked it.

Not that it was going to be easy, by any means.

Lily drew back slightly and tipped her head up to his, cautioning softly, "Reporters could show up here by tomorrow morning, hoping to get a comment from me."

He studied her protectively. "You need someone to run interference?"

Lily offered a shaky nod. "And maybe get Lucas out the back door without being seen or accosted by reporters."

As it happened, by six the next morning, there was one news truck in front of Lily's house, setting up. Within half an hour, two more showed up. So she went out the front and told everyone she'd have an official statement and mini press conference for them at eleven o'clock at the town hall, while Gannon and Lucas slipped out the back, through her neighbor's hedge and onto the next street over, where he had parked his truck.

Lucas got to preschool with no problem.

Lily went straight to Liz's office, arriving about the same time as Gannon and the rest of her family.

Everyone was upset. Especially her parents. "The stuff they're posting on the messages board at the news station and all the sports websites is just awful!" Violet declared. "The gist of the rumors is that this is all about money... That Lily is trying to shake Bode down for more..."

"Now, everyone who knows the facts of the case is aware that isn't true," Gannon muttered.

All turned to him in surprise.

The gleam in his eyes was formidable. "I've read the file. I know, as well as probably everyone in this room, that Lily never asked Bode for one cent of child support."

Silence fell. Family members nodded.

"But, as it happens, it doesn't matter whether a mother wants a father's financial assistance or not. The state of Texas feels any and all fathers should be fiscally accountable for their offspring," Gannon continued firmly, with that same look of utter concentration and ruthless determination he had whenever he talked law. "So once paternity was established, Bode was deemed responsible for his son. The court awarded Lucas a sum based on what Bode would earn in a regular job, post pro-football career."

He paused again, looking at one and all, before nodding reverently at Lily. "Lily easily could have fought that decision. Legally, her son was entitled to enjoy the same standard of living with his mother that he would have enjoyed with his father—at the time support was awarded." As they locked eyes, his gaze gentled. "She didn't do that."

"For good reason," Lily interjected, turning back to her folks. "I didn't want things getting complicated unnecessarily." She hadn't wanted to see stuff like this happening. Hadn't wanted it all to come down to money.

"Someone should speak out on behalf of Lily and make sure the public at large knows all of this," Jackson McCabe said.

Lily could see her handsome and accomplished physician father was more than ready to do it. Which, in her view, would only make things worse. She cut in, angry now. "No. The financial arrangements are no one else's business."

"But we have to do something!" Lily's mom said, upset. Like Lily's dad, Lacey was wearing blue hospital scrubs. "The things Bode implied in that interview just aren't true!"

Gannon and Liz exchanged lawyerly looks. Eventually, Gannon said, "If you go back and listen carefully to the interview, you'll see how carefully parsed Bode's actual words were. He implied he didn't like his son not having his last name. He never actually said anyone prevented that from happening. Just that he didn't want to fight Lily on anything more at that point."

"But people are going to assume it's all Lily's fault that Bode has no real relationship with his son," Rose declared with the heightened emotional state of someone who had also been through an ugly split with her ex.

"And that could very well hurt Lily politically when the next election rolls around again," her sister Violet—who was also in surgical scrubs—said.

Liz motioned for everyone to calm down. "Not if we release a carefully crafted statement in return. And impress upon everyone who is close to Lily and Lucas what a delicate situation this is right now, and ask them to *please not to talk to the press*."

Her family quickly got on board. "We can do that," they all said. A discussion ensued about who would call whom. Finally, they all filed out.

"This will all blow over before you know it," Liz soothed. She glanced at her watch. In the reception area, more doors opened and shut, and voices could be heard as her next clients arrived.

Gannon offered, "I'll help Lily with the statement."

"Thanks." Liz sighed her relief, then looked at Lily. "You're in good hands," she promised.

Funny, Lily thought that, too.

"YOU SURE YOU want to do this?" Gannon asked two hours later, before Lily walked into the media room at town hall.

She nodded. As always, she felt stronger with Gannon by her side. "I think it will go better if I read the statement to the press myself. That way, the reporters will get some film of me. Otherwise they'll be chasing me around." And that she did not want.

Gannon gave her shoulders a comforting squeeze. "Just touch your nose if you want me to step in."

"Will do." Lily walked out, Gannon staying just behind her.

Flashes began going off. Television cameras recorded her every move.

Her former political rival, Rex Carter, lingered in the background. Doing his best, it seemed to Lily, to make her nervous.

It didn't work.

No stranger to either crowds or the press, Lily stepped up to the podium. Smiled. "Thank you all for coming." She made eye contact with each and every journalist in the room. "First of all, I'd like to invite everyone to the First Annual Chili Cook-Off and Festival on Valentine's Day weekend. The festivities start with a parade tomorrow morning and conclude with a special dance on Saturday night. The proceeds are going to fund expansions of our library, the children's wing at the hospital and many other local charities. So you all bring your valentines and have a great time!"

Lily smiled again, feeling even more composed as the press event went on. "On a more personal note, I'd like to say that I wish Bode Daniels the best of luck in the continuation of his football career. I have always welcomed him in our son's life and always will." She paused to let her words sink in. "Currently, Bode and I are trying to work out the details of a new custody arrangement that will better serve us all. We'll let you know when there is something to announce. In the meantime, we would appreciate the time and the privacy to make this happen."

"Did you ask Bode Daniels to be the head judge and the grand marshal at the chili cook-off?" a reporter shouted.

Again, Lily maintained her composure. "Actually, I think we have former mayor and steering committee member Rex Carter to thank for that exciting development. I see him at the back of the room." She gestured magnanimously, for once glad the good old boy was on her heels. "Rex, how about you come up here and tell the folks a little about how this all transpired?"

His chest puffed out importantly, Rex made his way through the throngs of press. He took the podium and the microphone gleefully.

Lily used the opportunity to deftly slip away though a side door that, thanks to the deputies standing by, no one else could use.

"Now what?" Gannon asked.

"Get me out of here," Lily said. "Pronto."

He hugged her close, seeming as glad to be there for her as she was to have him. "You got it."

Chapter Twelve

"So what next?" Gannon asked when they had successfully slipped out of town hall, via the service entrance, and made their way to his pickup truck.

The chilly air and sunshine overhead invigorated Lily. She was so glad to be away from the crush of reporters. So glad to be alone with Gannon again. Forcing herself to get back into mayor mode, she waited for him to hit the unlock button on his keypad. "I'd like to head out to the county fairgrounds and see how things are going there. I especially want to see how the fire statue survived the move to the exhibition hall yesterday."

He moved to her side, opening the passenger door. Then he gave her a hand up into the cab, assisting her as gallantly as if they'd been on a date. "Actually," he said, smiling at her intimately, "I'd like to get a look at that, too."

Minutes later, they were standing in front of the glass display case that held the fire-roasted ceramic chili pepper.

Lily stared at the original work of art, thoroughly amazed. "I guess this just proves that context is everything," she said. What had seemed awkwardly out of place sitting on the grass of the town square looked incredibly delicate and lifelike under the lights.

Gannon stepped up to the glass. He shook his head, marveling, "It looks incredible, doesn't it? As though it—"

"—belongs here?" Lily finished his sentence for him.

Gannon nodded. He turned to Lily, his presence as evoc-
ative as the gentlest caress. He reached over and briefly
squeezed her hand before letting her go once again. "This is
what my mother should have been doing all along."

Trying not to read too much into his casual gesture, Lily
guessed his meaning. "Instead of being an art teacher?"

"Yeah." Gannon exhaled.

Their gazes locked, and they shared another moment of
tingling awareness. Finally, Gannon cleared his throat, regret tautening his handsome face. "If my mom had just followed her bliss..."

Knowing what it was to be in such a conundrum, and
make—in retrospect—what certainly seemed like the wrong
decision, Lily moved closer still. "Has your mom ever said
she regrets the compromises she made?"

Gannon inclined his head. "On the contrary." He rocked
back on his heels and tenderly searched Lily's eyes. "She's
very glad she had the time with me and my dad. And she
enjoyed all the years teaching. She says her students taught
her more than she ever taught them."

"Not in every case." Lily laughed and gestured at herself
self-deprecatingly. "I mean, I have no talent artistically. Of
all my siblings, only my sister Poppy has that. But your mom
opened up the world to me when I took her art survey class
in high school."

Gannon nodded. "A lot of people have told me they feel
that way. Which just goes to show, a person can have a positive impact anywhere they go if they choose to do so."

The sentiment in his low tone caught her attention. "Are
we talking about your mom now, or you?"

For a second, Lily thought he would not answer. Then
he turned to her and said, "I always thought that I would
be happy as long as I didn't compromise when it came to
my career."

"And now?" Lily asked, her pulse picking up.

Gannon looked deep into her eyes. "Being back in Laramie, spending time with you and Lucas, has made me realize there's still more to be had."

"Like family," she guessed.

"And a long-lasting relationship to anchor that family." Gannon exhaled. "The question is, how do you make that happen and still juggle all the responsibilities that come from being a partner and department head in a law firm, and not let anyone down?"

Lily gestured helplessly. "I don't know. My parents both have demanding careers as physicians, and they've always found a way to make it all work, but there are sacrifices to be made. Career opportunities they didn't take, or times they missed out on with us kids."

"And yet they've always been happy."

"Very much so."

He squeezed her hand encouragingly. "Maybe we'll figure it out, as well."

Amazingly, Lily was beginning to feel that, too. She smiled. "I hope so. In the meantime, we both have work to do…"

Lily resumed looking at the sculpture, and went back to the dilemma at hand. "I know Emmett Briscoe said he wanted this for his museum in Fort Worth, but I really think it belongs here."

Gannon held up a halting palm, not about to get in the middle. "You'll have to talk to him—and my mother—about that."

Lily's enthusiasm skyrocketed. "Do you think we could do that now?"

"I don't see why not." Gannon tried his mom on his cell, to no avail. "She's probably working in her studio. She doesn't have a phone out there."

Lily really wanted to get this settled. "Do you think she'd mind if we dropped by?"

Gannon pressed a light hand to her spine and escorted her in the direction of the exit. "Not at all."

They walked out of the exhibition hall side by side. Although the major festival preparation would not begin until six that evening when most of the locals had gotten off work, the grounds were already a beehive of activity as town workers strung red-and-white welcome banners across the entrance-way to the fairgrounds and set up the reviewing stand next to the entrance where the parade would end. Folding banquet tables were being brought in. Boxes upon boxes of cups and napkins, paper plates and silverware were delivered.

Miss Mim came toward the two of them excitedly. "I just heard the weather report!" she said. "It's going to be beautiful—sixty and sunny—both days!"

Lily beamed and hugged the committee chairwoman. "I'll be back at six to help get the concession stands set up for tomorrow."

"Count on me, too," Gannon said.

"All right, dears, see you then!" Miss Mim bustled back to supervise the crew.

Lily and Gannon climbed back into his pickup and drove out to the Triple M Ranch. And there, they received their second surprise of the day.

The one hundred acres immediately surrounding the Triple M Ranch house had been left untouched. The rest of the four hundred acres had been cordoned off into what appeared to be roughly forty ten-acre plots using a rainbow of different-colored surveying tapes to further delineate the lots. On the doorstep of the ranch was a gift box, courtesy of Rex Carter & Associates. Inside was a mock-up of what the subdivision was going to look like from the Triple M Ranch house porch, once it was built out.

"The houses are gorgeous," Lily said. "Million-dollar homes, every last one of them."

Gannon stared. "And my mom will be living in the middle of a subdivision?"

"You weren't aware this was how it was going to be set up?"

He grimaced. "Rex assured me that we—I mean my

mom—would still have her privacy as well as a beautiful view. That it would look like a series of small ranches, accessed in the usual way—"

"Directly off the country road."

Gannon nodded. "And that the homes would be set in their natural terrain. Instead, he's designed a grand entrance, is flattening and clearing the land, adding tennis courts and an Olympic-size swimming pool. Plus, he's added a lot of streets and cul-de-sacs—to the point you'll eventually need a traffic light to get out of there."

"I agree. There are a lot of changes. But what does this matter to you, since you'll be living in Fort Worth?"

"Because it's not what Rex and I agreed upon. And I still plan to come back here."

"To visit."

He nodded with his customary determination. "And when I do, I want it to be the way it was when I was growing up. Beautiful. Quiet. Peaceful."

"Just smaller."

"A place where I can get in touch with my roots."

Lily tried not to read too much into the sudden reverence in his voice. It wasn't as if Gannon were thinking of moving back to Laramie or anything. He liked his job and his life in Fort Worth. He wasn't a person who compromised on that. Ever. Any more than he was willing to compromise on what he still wanted in Laramie County.

Forcing herself to put her own foolish wishes aside, Lily swallowed hard. "Still, with forty new homes being put on the property, you knew there would be changes," she pointed out softly. "That it was going to have to look and feel a lot different."

Just as I know you are leaving in four more days.

"Knowing it and actually seeing it are two separate things," Gannon muttered unhappily.

Wasn't that the truth, Lily thought on a beleaguered sigh.

Maybe he wasn't the only one who needed to brace himself for what was coming next.

Harriett joined them on the front porch. She looked at her son. "I wondered what you were going to think of this when you saw it." Her own displeasure evident, the artist pointed to the soon-to-be drastically altered view. "You don't like it any more than I do, do you?"

Gannon said nothing.

But then, Lily noted, he didn't have to.

Nor, for that matter, did she.

WITH THE REPORTERS GONE, and his mom agreeing to at least think about leaving her fire statue with the town of Laramie, as originally planned, Gannon drove Lily back to work.

She was unusually quiet en route.

Which, given all she had to have on her mind, was not really a surprise, so Gannon fell silent, too. It had been a hell of a shock, seeing what Rex Carter and his associates had planned for his former childhood home. Even though he knew some changes had to be made, for practical and financial reasons, he still hated to see the feel of the Triple M Ranch lost. Hated the thought that soon he would be leaving Lily—again. As well as her son, whom was quickly becoming very fond of. Not to mention the glimpse of family she had provided him the past few days.

He realized now that he needed more from life than he'd been getting.

He wanted Lily—and Lucas—to be part of that, even if it was in a long-distance-relationship kind of way.

Whether or not Lily would agree to that, however, was something else entirely.

Meanwhile, there were mounting problems back at the firm that needed his attention.

A clamor of people asking he return to Fort Worth sooner rather than later. And precious little time to work on his chief goal of further cementing his relationship with Lily before he had to leave town again. Because there was one thing he was very sure about—he wanted their love affair to continue. So when they reached the town hall, Gannon snagged her forearm before she could emerge from the vehicle.

Grinning, he reeled her playfully back to his side and watched her blush.

Appreciating how pretty and mayor-like she looked in her trim blue sheath dress, jacket and matching heels, her honey-blond hair tucked into a classy chignon at the nape of her neck, he asked, "Do you have plans tonight?"

Elegant brow furrowing, she touched the long strand of pearls around her neck. "Besides working at the fairgrounds?" she inquired, regarding him with the same cautious cool she had used at the press conference earlier in the day.

So this was going to be harder than he thought. That was okay; he liked a challenge. And he especially liked her.

"What about dinner?" he inquired casually. *Besides hopefully spending it with me?*

She flashed him a droll look. "A food truck is bringing that for all the volunteers."

He stroked the inside of her wrist and felt her quiver. "Good to know."

She extricated her hand from his and regarded him contemplatively. "I was planning to eat there with everyone else, but I could sit with you then on a break."

This was beginning to sound like high school. Except high school, Gannon thought, had never been this much fun. Back then, he had never wanted anyone anywhere near as much as he wanted Lily.

And the truth was, because of their three years' age difference, he'd barely known her in high school. "I'll take you up on that," he said, lamenting all the lost opportunities of the past and vowing there would be no more.

His gaze drifted over her. His body responded. "What about after?"

Lily hesitated. "I don't think there's going to be an after. The work will probably go to midnight. And we start really early tomorrow when the contestants come in to register and set up and all that. Not to mention the parade tomorrow at lunchtime…"

"Take a breath."

"Sorry." She pressed her fingers to her temples. "I feel stressed. So many people are counting on this, and I really want it to go well."

He leaned closer, inhaling the freesia of her perfume. "You've certainly had a lot of publicity."

"That we have." Lily briefly shut her eyes. "Between Bode's antics and the hullaballoo over the fire statue, I don't think there's anyone in the entire state who doesn't know about the chili festival on Valentine's Day weekend."

Gannon wondered if she had any idea how much she affected him. How much he wanted to haul her into his arms, take her to bed and sleep with her all night long. "What about Lucas? Is he okay with you being gone so much?"

Surprise at his question mingled briefly with the regret in her eyes. "Lucas is having a sleepover at my parents' house with his triplet cousins for the next three nights in a row," she said wryly. "So with the party atmosphere my folks have planned, I doubt he will even miss me."

Gannon smiled. If there was one thing the McCabe clan understood, it was how to pitch in as a family. "Sounds as though he will have a fun time," he agreed.

Lily rubbed her finger across the fabric of her sheath, stretched taut across her slender thighs. "And then there's my ex, too," she ruminated on a weary exhalation of breath. "Bode has already texted me that he wants to see Lucas the moment he arrives tomorrow."

"With or without photographers?" Gannon deadpanned.

Lily rolled her eyes.

"Plus, I plan to take Lucas around between my own scheduled appearances. So between all of that," she said, looking slightly more content, "I imagine Lucas will get plenty of attention." She put her hand on the door latch.

Gannon jumped out of the truck and walked around to assist her. "Just so you know," he said, holding the door for her, "I'm available, too."

She peered up at him thoughtfully. "Thanks. I may take you up on that."

He grinned. "Looking forward to it. And, Lily…" They could be seen by anyone going in or out of town hall, so he resisted the urge to take her all the way in his arms and instead contented himself with a brief squeeze of her hand. "I don't think I've told you," he said huskily, "but you look incredibly beautiful today."

"IT WAS A COMPLIMENT, and a nice one at that. I don't understand why you're so upset," Violet said when she came by on a break from the hospital to see if there was anything she could do to help Lily.

Lily moved away from her computer, where she had been writing her opening remarks for the celebration, and went back to bundling brochures. "Because he meant it."

Violet rolled her eyes and moved to lend a hand. "Do you know what I would give to have a man in my life who would pay that much attention to me?"

Lily plucked more brochures from the printer's shipping box. "You have guys who are interested in you."

"None like Sterling."

Her fiancé's death had hit her hard. Particularly since in the end, there had been so little she could do, even as a physician, to help. "You'll find someone else," Lily soothed.

"Like you have?" Violet snapped a rubber band around another bundle.

Lily flushed guiltily.

"Come on, Lily," her sister chided. "You're head over heels…"

Lily blushed. "In lust with him."

Silence fell. "That's it?" a disbelieving Violet asked finally.

"It's all it can be."

Violet shook her head. "Now you're beginning to sound like Poppy."

Who they all knew was in love with her best friend, a career soldier deployed in the Middle East, but just wouldn't admit that anything else would ever be possible.

Violet walked over to hug her. "You have an opportunity here, Lily. Don't blow it."

Lily thought about her sister's advice the rest of the afternoon. And she was still thinking about it when she met up with the rest of the volunteers at the county fairgrounds.

Gannon was easy to spot.

He was surrounded by single women all clamoring for his attention. With his hair rumpled, his tall body clad in a muscle-molding knit shirt and jeans, he looked sexy as could be. Watching, Lily felt a pang of jealousy twist in her heart. Maybe it was foolish, but she wanted him to be all hers. And no one else's. Not now. Not ever.

He walked over and, not caring that there were a lot of other people watching, gave her a one-armed hug and a kiss to her temple.

Not sure she was ready to go public with their "whatever kind of relationship this was" yet, Lily immediately drew back. Blushed furiously. Then put her hands on her hips and asked in a commanding tone, "Do you know where Miss Mim is?"

Totally unrepentant, he flashed a grin as big as all of Texas. "Actually, she assigned you to work with me."

Lily groaned. It was hard enough as it was to keep her feelings under wraps, and now she was going to be in forced proximity with him! "Did you arrange that?"

"Didn't have to," he drawled. "Miss Mim thought of it all on her own."

Fighting off the thrill Gannon generated whenever he was

near, Lily shut her eyes. Then, biting down on an oath, she forced herself to look back up at him. "She's matchmaking!"

Gannon leaned forward to whisper in Lily's ear, "Works for me." His hand slid around her back, caressing gently. "And it should work for you, too."

Something was working within her—that was for sure. It did not matter anymore how risky it was, or how impractical. She wanted to be with Gannon, more than ever. For them both to be all in—to each other. And she preferred it to be without either a cheering section or an audience, which was, as they all knew, pretty much impossible in a small town, where anonymity was definitely not the order of the day.

Fortunately for everyone's sake, she and Gannon had no more time for flirting, given all that had to be done and the long list of chores Miss Mim had assigned them.

For the next two hours, Lily and Gannon worked together setting up a long line of shade awnings. They unloaded tables and folding chairs and arranged them to make an outdoor cafeteria beneath a pavilion. Meanwhile, others worked on opening up and cleaning the wooden booths the food vendors would use.

Lily and Gannon were about to break for dinner when Lily's sister Rose came to get them. "There are some organizational problems. Miss Mim wants you and Gannon in the fairgrounds office, pronto."

THERE WAS A heated argument going on between members of the steering committee when they arrived. Not surprisingly, Rex Carter was at the center of it.

Miss Mim turned to Gannon. "Have you stepped down as grand marshal and head judge?"

He shrugged his broad shoulders affably. "Not officially, but if that's what you all need me to do, I'm happy to comply."

Marybeth Simmons stepped in. "We can't ask Gannon to do that for one of Rex's rogue ideas, especially since it was announced weeks ago that Gannon is the grand marshal."

The local PTA president turned to look at one and all. "I think we should stick with that."

Lulu Sanderson interjected with the savvy of a barbecue-chain heiress and adept businesswoman, "Except that it's also been announced that Bode Daniels is going to be the grand marshal and head judge, too." She looked at one and all. "We really don't want to be accused of false advertising."

"Maybe we should let Bode head up the parade and Gannon be the chief food critic," Erin Monroe-Wheeler said. "Or vice versa."

"Not sure that's such a good idea," Rex muttered, tipping his black Resistol back on his head.

Everyone turned to him.

Rex tugged at the string tie around his neck. "Well, given the fact that they're both romantically involved with Lily in one way or another," he said.

Lily choked. "Excuse me?" She felt herself flushing fire-engine red.

Rex squared his shoulders. "You have a son with one, and whatever is going on now with the other guy. Sorry, Gannon, but it's obvious to one and all you two have the hots for each other. And that, uh, might be too complicated a situation for the public at large."

To Lily's consternation, Gannon wasn't the least bit upset that their attraction to each other was becoming a matter of public record. At least so far as members of the steering committee were concerned.

He stepped in, completely composed. "It'll be fine," he told everyone calmly. "Bode and I will split the duties as we see fit. Or whatever works…"

Talk continued a little while longer. Finally, it was decided not to make too big a deal of it. After all, Bode could be so swamped with press attention he wouldn't be able to do the chili festival justice, and that was what they all wanted and needed most: the event to run smoothly so as many funds as possible could be raised for the various community projects underway.

"Are you really okay with sharing the limelight the next couple of days?" Lily asked later, when the evening's events were wrapping up.

Gannon walked her as far as her SUV. Despite the rigorous activities of the evening, he still looked full of energy, not to mention handsome as all get-out in his flannel shirt and shearling jacket. "It could get awkward," Lily persisted.

He raised his brow. "As if it already hasn't been."

She nodded. "Point taken."

Silence fell.

He stayed where he was, not touching her, clearly wanting to. His gaze drifted over her face. "It's still early."

For what? Lily glanced at her watch, thinking she should be completely worn out, but wasn't. "Nearly eleven."

He shrugged, still looking as if he wanted to kiss her again. "There are a couple places in town that stay open late…"

All places where they would be seen together and commented on, once assumptions were made.

Of course, people would still talk if they sought a quieter sanctuary. But at least then no one would know exactly what was being said. Or in what manner. And since his family ranch was out of the question…

Lily hitched in a breath and whispered, "You really want to come back to my place, don't you?"

He locked gazes with her and sauntered closer, looking as relaxed about what was happening between them as she wanted to be. "Shows, hmm?" He rubbed his thumb across the curve of her lower lip.

Lily knew a lot was riding on her attitude. "You understand you won't be staying long?"

The corners of the mouth that had given her such unbelievable pleasure quirked up in a self-deprecating smile. "I'm okay with whatever you want tonight."

And that seemed to be, in his view anyway, more time alone together. To kiss and make love and further whatever this turned out to be between them. The question was, what did she want? More passion? An enduring friendship? A simple love affair? Assuming anything between her and Gannon could ever be uncomplicated.

Or enough of a boundary to keep her from sacrificing her whole heart into a future that was not likely to happen? At least not the way she wanted it to materialize.

Lily did not know.

And yet, the moment they walked into her house, the intimacy surrounded them. Gannon looked around while she turned on a light. "It's quiet."

Lily nodded. There were times when she would think it was too quiet—without Lucas. Not tonight. Tonight it seemed just right.

She reached up to Gannon and stroked his jaw. "It always is when Lucas is with my folks."

He nodded soberly, looking deep into her eyes. "I like quiet," he said softly.

Lily said to heck with protecting herself. Rose on tiptoe. Circled her arms about his neck and guided his head down to hers. "And I," she looked at him gently, tenderly, "like you."

THOSE WEREN'T EXACTLY the words Gannon had been waiting to hear, but he supposed the declaration was something. Especially since she had spent most of the past few days drawing him maddeningly close, then pushing him abruptly away.

He went still, waiting to see what she would do.

For a second, he thought she was going to change her mind and ask him to leave. Then something in her expression changed, and her guard lowered. A faint smile tugging at her lips, she went up on tiptoe. Eyes shuttering closed, she pressed her lips to his. Wantonly. Hotly. Then sweetly and tenderly.

Passion swept through him, the need to make her his

stronger than ever. "If you want me to leave," he murmured, luxuriating in the soft silky feel of her, "you're going to have to kick me out of here—now."

Lily shook her head, already unbuttoning his shirt. "You can stay." She stroked her hands across his chest and kissed him again. "So long as you realize," she murmured, her lips blazing a trail down his throat, "this is only a temporary thing." Her hand went to his fly. "For as long as you're in town."

He swept her into his arms and carried her up the stairs, to her bed. "Or longer..."

She gasped as he gently set her down. "Gannon..."

He kicked off his boots, bent to tug off hers, then dropped them on the floor and stretched out beside her. A softly glowing night-light and the moonlight shining in through the windows provided the only illumination in the room. He rolled so she was beneath him and kissed her hard and soft and every way in between, aware she was everything he had ever wanted in a woman and more.

"I'm not going to put limits on my feelings or wants and needs, Lily." He slid his hands beneath her sweater, finding one taut nipple, then the other. He lowered his head, breathing in the scent of her, letting his lips follow his palms. "And neither," he whispered as her head fell back and she arched up against him, making a tiny little whimpering sound that sent his senses swimming, "should you..."

Lily hadn't meant to end up making love. Again. Hadn't meant to be so reckless. But she couldn't seem to help herself.

There was just something about him that drew her to him like nothing and no one else.

Something that made her let down her defenses and open up her heart. A connection that made her go all fluid and warm.

He'd been so kind to her, so good to her son.

He tasted so good, so undeniably male.

As his hands slid down her hips and he pulled her against him, she felt him, hard with need.

All her life she had longed to be wanted the way he desired her. The surprise was that she needed him, too. Not just this way, their bodies pressed intimately together, but emotionally, as well. As his hands moved over her, undressing, caressing, she gave him full rein. He took her with the hunger and need she possessed.

Afterward, they cuddled close. Gannon stroked a hand down her back. Pressed kisses in her hair. "What is it?"

How did he always know? Lily asked herself. Finally, she whispered, "You don't want me to answer that."

He shifted so she was beneath him. Framing her face with his big hands, he looked down at her, his expression serious. "Tell me," he urged.

Lily swallowed at the rough note of possession in his voice. "I don't want to use you to make myself feel better."

"So what are you saying exactly?" He nudged his knee playfully between the two of hers. "You want to use me to make yourself feel *worse*?"

She laughed despite herself and felt a melting sensation in her middle as he settled in the cradle of her thighs. With effort, she tried not to make too much of her fears. "My life is a mess right now."

He favored her with a sexy half smile, his gaze roving her face. "Good thing I'm here, then." He bent his head and kissed her again.

Lily moaned. Much more of this, and she'd end up falling in love with him. If she wasn't already! Her hands clasped his shoulders tightly. "You're confusing me even more."

Smug male confidence exuded from him in mesmerizing waves. "And here all I really wanted to do was turn you on."

She gasped as he found her breasts. "Gannon."

He laved her nipples with his tongue, then blew them dry. "You like that?"

As their eyes met, and the air reverberated with escalating passion, Lily nodded. "Sooo much."

"Good." He made his way down her ribs, to her belly button, lower still. "What about this?"

Her thighs fell apart. She trembled. "Awfully nice, too."

"And this?"

Her knees went weak as he took her into his mouth, drawing deep. Making her want more and more.

She panted. "Spectacular." She shuddered as his fingers found their way inside her.

"But…" She gasped as he kissed her again, deeply and erotically. She tore her lips from his. "Being the equality-minded woman I am, I think I should have a turn to do whatever I want, too." She flipped him onto his back.

He obliged with a slow, sexy smile. "You think so?"

"Oh, yeah…" She explored the velvety smooth heat and hardness.

He exhaled. "Nice…"

"And this?"

He shifted again, so she was astride him. "Even sweeter."

Hands cupping her hips, he positioned her intimately.

"And this?" Lily continued stroking.

He set her down, slowly, patiently, until she was teetering on the edge of something even more wonderful, hot and aching inside. Lily sighed. "More than enough to make me want you all over again."

"Good," Gannon whispered as even more moisture flowed. He penetrated her slowly, ardently cupping her buttocks and stroking the insides of her thighs as she opened herself up to him even more. "Because I will never stop wanting you…"

"Oh, Gannon, I want you, too…" Lily whispered back, kissing him with all the tenderness and passion she held in her heart.

I want you in my life. Not just for now. But forever.

Chapter Thirteen

Lily blinked, not sure she'd heard right. "Bode brought his own parade float?"

Lulu Sanderson shrugged. "I gather it was Rex Carter's idea." The barbecue heiress motioned Lily over to the street behind Main to see it.

The monstrosity her ex had carted in was large enough to be in a big-city holiday parade. Done all in white, the semitrailer-size platform on wheels easily dwarfed every other convertible, stagecoach and farm wagon lined up to be in the celebration. It sported twin thrones for Bode and Viviana—both of whom were dressed in designer slacks and shirts made in Dallas Gladiator team colors. And a small block, like a bench seat, was situated just in front of them.

It was pretty over-the-top, all right, Lily decided. And suddenly her Friday morning, which had already been fraught with a steady stream of unforeseen snafus, just got a whole lot worse.

And that was a shame, she thought wistfully. Because Thursday evening had been so incredibly nice…all the way until dawn, when Gannon had had to head back to his own place to shower and change clothes.

But now it was out of romantic fantasyland and back to reality, she told herself sternly as the PTA president joined in the fray.

"I just talked to Bode's entourage. They want his float to

go first," a harried-looking Marybeth Simmons told Lily. "And you know that can't be the case. The fire department and the Veterans' color guard always lead the way. But they are insisting that because their float is so large, it should go right after the banner!"

Lily really did not want to have to be the one who made this decision. Where was Gannon when she needed him?

Talking to a group of single ladies, of course, helping move a few big food containers around.

Not that it was his fault he was so handsome.

And helpful.

With a sigh, Lily turned back to Marybeth and Lulu. "Where's Miss Mim?"

"Supervising the setups for the wings and ribs cooking competitions being held today."

Bode walked toward her, decked out in the usual Gladiator jersey and hat and jeans, and some very fancy, very expensive boots—also embroidered with his team jersey number and colors. "Hey, Lily."

She braced herself to be the one saying what he probably did not want to hear. "Hey, Bode. I wanted to—"

He lifted a hand to interrupt. "I know I have to judge the food and stuff all day, but I want to spend time with Lucas this evening. So—" he paused to look her in the eye "—can you get him to me about six?"

Lily noted her ex looked sincere in his desire to be with his son. The ever-present anxiety she felt these days faded just a little bit. "Sure," she returned amicably. "Where do you want to meet?"

Bode shoved a hand through his cropped hair and looked around at the people already angling to get a moment of his time the minute he and Lily finished. "Wherever you think would be best."

Glad she did not have his level of fame to contend with, Lily said, "How about the fairgrounds office? It's on the second floor in the exhibition building."

"I'll be there," Bode promised, just as quietly. "In the meantime—" he handed her a tyke-size Gladiators jersey with his number emblazoned on the back "—do you think you could get Lucas to wear this today?"

Of course they had to be color coordinated.

Hard to believe she had ever dated this guy, never mind borne a child with him. "Sure," Lily said politely, resolved to be conciliatory for all their sakes.

Viviana, the three nannies she'd met before and Lucas's two baby sisters joined them. Gorgeous as ever, Viviana looked at Lily, then her husband. Which prompted Bode to shove his hand through his hair again and say, "Listen, we want Lucas to ride on our float with us, too."

And what a photo op that would make, Lily thought drolly. Five of the most gorgeous people on earth…

Just one big happy family.

She eyed the huge float, her mind now solely on safety. "Where is Lucas going to be?"

Bode replied, "We figured he'd sit on the bench, between the two thrones."

So Lucas would be front and center.

"Who's going to hold him?" Her question was met with a hapless shrug. Forced to be the bad guy, she said, "I'm serious, Bode. I don't want Lucas getting excited and jumping up and running around and tumbling off." As four-year-old boys were inclined to do.

"There's a wall along the side that will keep him contained," he pointed out, ever the invincible jock.

"It's still a moving vehicle." Without a safety harness in sight.

Bode floundered, for the first time looking completely out of his depth. "Ah, well, Viviana wanted us each to hold one of the girls on our laps…"

Okay, then… "Can you hold one of your daughters and Lucas comfortably on your lap for the entire parade route—which will likely take a little under an hour?"

Bode hesitated.

Lily lost patience. "Maybe you should ask your wife."

"Fine. I'll do that." Bode strode off. A heated discussion followed. Well, Lily amended, watching covertly, heated on *Viviana's* part. Bode mostly listened with a stoic expression on his face. Eventually, he came back. "Maybe you have a point. It might be a little dangerous having all three kids up there at once." He paused and shot a look at his ever-present public relations team, who were busy chatting up the local dignitaries. "I guess we can get photos of all five of us together when the fair atmosphere is in full swing."

Lily nodded and tried not to think ill of him. "I think that would be best."

Bode left again.

A few sports reporters from the region went over to talk to him. While he was still holding court with them, Gannon joined Lily. He caught her by the hand and tugged her into a narrow corridor that led to the alley between Main and Second streets. "Looking a little stressed out."

Lily shoved her bangs off her face. "I'm feeling a lot stressed out."

He studied her intently. "Because…?"

"Bode and that whole mess."

Looking ready to take action against her opponents, he turned her hand palm up and rubbed his thumb along her lifeline. "What else?" he asked, his voice husky soft.

The fact I've thrown out a lifetime of common sense and made love with you on three separate occasions in the past week. And, given my choice, I'd be making love to you again. Whenever we could.

But this was not the time to be talking about her romantic ambivalence or worry that this would all turn out to be just a temporary fling, so Lily forced herself to get back to the business at hand.

"Festival stuff," she said finally.

"Such as?"

Lily shrugged. "It looks as though you'll be riding in the grand marshal car alone."

He chuckled over the marching bands tuning up in the distance. "Gee, I'm really disappointed about that."

On the streets behind them, there were a lot of people—more than expected—parking and getting out of cars. "Although," she teased back, "I could probably get Rex Carter to ride in the convertible with you."

Gannon vetoed that with a single shake of his head. Using his grip on her hand as leverage, he tugged her closer still. Looking as if he wanted nothing more than to have his way with her then and there, he cupped her chin in his hand and impishly searched her eyes. "Sure you don't want to ride with me?"

Wouldn't that make people talk—even more than they already were! Lily stepped back, putting a more proper distance between them. Turning, she headed for Main, leaving him no choice but to follow along behind her. "Thanks, but I'm going to be hosting all the local dignitaries in the viewing stand." She tossed a glance over her shoulder and found him behind her, avidly admiring the view.

Telling herself she was woman enough to handle that, too, Lily sassed back, "You can wave at me when you pass, if you like."

He winked. "Only if you wave back."

Lily stepped out onto the sidewalk. They were standing in front of Jenna Lockhart's Bridal Salon, which was closed for the day. She turned her glance away from the beautiful gowns on display in the plate glass window that she would likely never have a chance to wear.

She swallowed. "We have to stop this. Or…"

Gannon's glance narrowed. "What?" he asked, serious now.

Lily used her clipboard like a shield. She regarded Gannon as matter-of-factly as if they were talking about the weekend weather forecast. "People will think…" she said with an officious smile.

He lifted a brow, caressing her not with his hand this time, but with his eyes. "We're falling in love?"

There he went, finishing her sentences for her again.

Correctly as it happened.

Knowing, however, this was not the time or the place to be having such a conversation, if there ever would be before he left town again, Lily drew a bolstering breath. Straightened her spine, and gave him an encouraging pat on the arm, even as she directed him to the waiting grand marshal convertible coupe. "Have fun out there."

She was going to do her best to achieve the same.

HOURS LATER, LILY glanced at her watch for the hundredth time since six o'clock had come—and gone.

In the corner of the fairgrounds office, Gannon sat with her son, patiently using unopened boxes of pencils, paper clips, pens and staples to build one structure after another. Office supplies that were only available to them because they had been left out on a shelf next to one of the desks.

Gannon—who'd had his own very full day, judging the food categories of ribs, barbecue and desserts—gave her a chiding look as she continued to pace back and forth. "Sure you don't want to sit down with us?"

Lily shook her head, continued pacing around the room. "Where *is* he?" she asked in frustration.

Gannon shrugged, as if Bode's no-show were no big deal. "Maybe he got caught up by fans or more reporters. They've been after him all day."

That was true—to the point that Viviana and their other two children and their nannies had sought sanctuary out of the public eye.

Gannon grinned as Lucas achieved a particularly difficult balancing act with paper clips and rulers. "Everyone wants to know what's going to happen with him and the Gladiators."

Also true.

As was the notion of how much better her son's life would be if only Gannon were her little boy's daddy instead of the famed QB.

Admiring Gannon's patience, Lily finally drew up a chair and sat down next to them, noting that Lucas was as relaxed as Gannon. "You're…sympathetic."

Gannon shrugged. "Situations like this are complicated, so I try not to judge. But you're right—" he checked out the time, too "—it is getting awfully late. Have you tried texting or calling him on his cell?"

Unease trickled through her. "Twice. No answer."

He kept his eyes on her face. "Want to page him on the PA system?"

Lily barely suppressed a moan. "Not unless you want a stampede."

"What about his wife?" he suggested helpfully. "Maybe she knows where he is."

Good point, but… "I don't have her number."

"His personal relations team?"

Lily tensed. "I'd rather not involve them."

He reached out and squeezed her hand, there for her, whether she wanted him to be or not. "Then we wait."

Lucas finally looked up, the fruit cup and milk she'd gotten him earlier all gone. "Mommy, I'm hungry."

"I know, sweetie."

His lower lip slid out as the confusion of the past week finally took its toll. "You said I'm supposed to have dinner with my daddy."

Lily did her best to reassure him. "That was the plan."

Her son's gaze grew watery. "Then where is he, Mommy?" Lucas asked, even more plaintively.

Good question.

Really good question.

After another twenty minutes had passed, Lily had to

admit Bode had either forgotten or gotten hung up somewhere. With someone else.

"Now can we eat?" Lucas asked again, his little body drooping with fatigue after his long and tiring day.

Lily nodded, suddenly feeling near tears herself. It had been one thing when Bode had disappointed her. But it broke her heart to see him letting their son down this way. Especially when Lucas had just now started to trust him.

While Lucas and Gannon deconstructed their creations and put the office supplies back where they belonged, Lily texted, Can't wait any longer. Taking Lucas to get some dinner.

"So what are you in the mood for?" she asked her son as they walked out into the hallway. "They've got hot dogs and cheeseburgers and chicken tenders—"

"Actually," Rose said as she intercepted Lily at the top of the stairs, "they may not. There are so many people here, all the concession stands are running out of food!"

"It's no problem," Jackson and Lacey said when Lily got hold of her parents via their cells and they arrived to pick up Lucas, who was happily sitting on Gannon's lap and eating one of the few items left in the concession stands—a funnel cake sprinkled with powdered sugar.

Lacey held out her arms for her grandson. "You're probably ready to go home and have a grilled cheese or peanut-butter-and-jelly sandwich anyway, aren't you?"

"And milk," Lucas said, his face covered with powdered sugar. "I like milk."

"Coming right up," Jackson promised.

"Thanks, Mom and Dad." Lily hugged both her parents.

"You just do your job," Lacey said. "We'll take care of Lucas. What time do you want him here tomorrow?"

Lily was so frazzled over the dinner debacle she couldn't think. "When do the pony rides start?"

Gannon accepted another hug from her son, then glanced at the schedule he'd downloaded to his phone. "9:00 a.m."

"Is that okay?" Lily asked her mom and dad.

"No problem," Lacey said. "We'll call you when we're on our way."

Lily said good-night to her son, then turned back to Gannon, who was standing there. The epitome of masculinity, he was as compassionate, kind and sexy as ever. "How do you feel about making a few calls to round up some extra food?"

He grinned and gave her a big hug. And kiss. "I'm all in."

AN HOUR LATER, thanks to frantic SOS's from all members of the chili cook-off committee and resultant cooperation from every restaurant in the area, the concession stands were once again serving Texas favorites of all kinds.

The fairgrounds were teeming with tourists, many of them football fans, on the lookout for Bode and his supermodel wife and kids. None of whom could be found.

But the country band hired to play that night had started. The twinkling red heart-shaped lights strung around the fairgrounds lent a festive Valentine's Day weekend air to the cooling night.

Gannon would have liked to haul Lily out onto the dance floor. But every time he got even close to doing so, something else happened that required her attention.

When it came to a work-related crisis, he considered himself a patient person. He understood she had a job to do. He admired her tenacity.

When it came to his personal life, he didn't want to put anything off unnecessarily. Or feel anywhere near as frustrated as he did at this moment.

Maybe it was selfish. He didn't care. He wanted to have Lily all to himself, so they could make the most of the previous little time they had left before he headed back to his own professional responsibilities.

And if it wasn't going to be during the dance…as it apparently wasn't, he noted as another opportunity to hold her in his arms came…and went…then it would be later…

Finally, around eleven, the band called it a night. The party began breaking up. He offered to drive her home. She was so tired, she agreed to leave her SUV at the fairgrounds and climbed into his pickup truck.

All too soon, Gannon parked in her driveway and watched the motion-detector lights on the outside of her bungalow come on. Suddenly, they were both bathed in a soft yellow glow. He drank her in, admiring her from head to toe. Despite the tumultuous events of the day, Lily looked as lovely as ever. She pushed out of the cab. He walked around to join her. Together, they walked into her house. "Looks as though the festival is a success."

"The first half of the festival is a success." She took off her jacket and reached for his. Both landed on the coatrack next to the door. "We have another day to go." She drew a deep breath, oblivious of the way the action raised and then lowered the soft swell of her breasts beneath the long-sleeved festival T-shirt.

Wishing he could just take her to bed and make love to her until all the weariness and uncertainty in her eyes went away, Gannon let his gaze rove the mussed strands of her honey-blond hair and said, "I predict tomorrow will be even better."

Holding on to the newel post, she toed off her fancy red cowgirl boots, then watched as he did the same with his boots.

She tilted her head. "Thank you for being here with me tonight."

Gannon knew they were both tired. He also knew their time together was dwindling. He gathered her close. "Don't you know there isn't anywhere else I'd rather be?" he said tenderly.

Her lips curved ruefully, even as her turquoise eyes shone with hope. "You're letting the romantic atmosphere go to your head," she teased.

He tunneled his hands in her hair and brought her face up to his. "Or my heart."

She rose on tiptoe, the softness of her body giving new heat and hardness to his. "Gannon…" she moaned wistfully, the urgent yearning on her face matching his.

He kissed her passionately, shifting her closer still. And still they kissed, until their tongues twined intimately and feelings poured from his heart, followed swiftly by a need that was soul deep.

Lily might not want to admit it yet, but no woman had ever touched him this way, and he was pretty sure, given the way she was kissing him back and pressing her soft, lithe body against his, that he did the same for her. If being in each other's arms like this wasn't heaven on earth, he didn't know what was.

He stroked his hands through her hair, moved them lower to ease beneath the hem of her shirt. She sighed as he caressed her silky breasts through the lace of her bra and breathed in the sweet feminine scent of her.

He grinned, bending to slip a hand beneath her knees. "This is what Valentine's Day is all about, Lily." Shifting her up into his arms and against his chest, he carried her up the stairs, down the hall to her bed. He set her down and began kissing her again.

She whimpered even as she kissed him back, threading her hands through his hair. "Exactly why it's dangerous." She guided him closer still. "Nights like this make me feel reckless."

Wanting her to see how right they were for each other— long-term—he began to undress her, then lowered her gently to her bed. "Reckless can be good." He disrobed, too, and stretched out beside her. She rolled onto her side and arced against him, her mouth as hungry as his, her breasts pressed against his chest, one of her thighs looped over top of his, giving him the kind of access he had longed to have.

He stroked and kissed, delving into her mouth with a

rhythm of penetration and retreat that was echoed by the searching caress of his hands. Until there was no doubt for either of them about what they wanted or what was coming next.

She trembled and caught his head in her hands as he found her breasts, suckled gently and then moved lower still.

"Gannon."

"Let your guard down, Lily. Let it down with me..." His own body throbbing, he explored the silky soft insides of her thighs, loving her slowly, thoroughly, until she was quivering from head to toe, shuddering and moaning low in her throat.

And still he wanted more.

Unable to get enough of her, he moved upward again, kissing her even more deeply and evocatively this time. Their tongues mated intimately, their slow searing kiss enough to send her sliding over the edge. She strained against him, convulsing, even as he wanted her all the more.

He moved as if to take her.

She laughed softly. "No. My turn..."

And then she was shimmying down his body. Loving every inch of him with her hands and lips and tongue. Using the palms of her hands to generate scorching heat that started across his pecs, she slid down his abdomen, found the insides of his thighs and the aching, throbbing length of him. The softness and skill of her lips created a firestorm of need. He reached for her, wanting her—now. Shifting her onto her back, he lifted her against him and surged inside.

Lily had wanted to be in command of not just their lovemaking but her feelings this evening. A hopeless aim, as it turned out. Every time he touched her, kissed her, every time he possessed her like this, she felt the strength of their passion. She felt it in his kisses, in the exquisite way their bodies melded and their hearts thundered in unison.

She might not know what the future held for them beyond the next two days. But she knew this. Right now, Gannon meant everything to her, and she urged him to go deeper, harder still. Until all reservations were put aside and they soared into a pleasure unlike anything they had ever experienced.

As they clung together, gasping, bodies reverberating in pleasure, Lily knew she was right where she wanted to be, now. And could be for the foreseeable future, if they found a way to curtail their recklessness. Remain patient and take the wonder they had found one slow, patient step at a time.

Chapter Fourteen

Gannon woke to the chiming sound of an alarm, with Lily still wrapped in his arms. She moaned and snuggled closer. Aware he had never felt as content as he did at this moment, he stroked a hand through the silk of her hair. "Want to sleep a little more?"

She rubbed her temple against his bare chest. Yawned. "You have no idea. But I have to get up and shower and get to my parents' place in time to have breakfast with Lucas before I head back to the fairgrounds." She released a breath. "It opens at 8:00 a.m. today so the contestants can start cooking their chili in time for the first round of judging, which begins at noon."

She had a point. He threw back the covers. "I better get a move on, too. I promised Clint McCulloch I'd help him transport the ponies to the fairgrounds."

She rose from the bed and stretched luxuriantly. "What time?"

He grinned as his body stirred in response. Damn, she was beautiful, with clothes and without. "I'm supposed to be at his ranch by seven."

Lily reached for her robe. "You want to shower here?"

Did he! "With you…?"

Mischief lit her eyes. "Then we'd both be late."

She was right about that. Whenever they started making love, they lost all track of time and place.

Lily glided closer and kissed him anyway—a down payment for later. Arms still wreathed about his neck, she eased back to look into his eyes and regarded him with mock innocence. "I meant in the hall bathroom while I use the master," she explained, letting him go.

Figuring he'd make up later tonight for their lack of time now, he drawled, "Thank you kindly, ma'am." He tipped an imaginary hat, then grabbed her wrist and reeled her back to his side.

Her eyes widened.

"Oh, and one more thing."

"Yes?" she asked.

He kissed the top of her head. "Save a dance for me tonight."

"YOU'RE LOOKING HAPPY this morning," Lily's mom said when she let herself in the back door.

And she was. More than she had ever dreamed possible.

Lily smiled. Though her parents were still in their pajamas, her son was already dressed in a Western shirt and vest, jeans and boots.

"I'm ready to ride the horses, Mommy!" he enthused.

Lily glanced at her watch. "I can see that. But the pony rides don't start until nine o'clock. I'm just here to have breakfast with you before I have to go to work. Grandma Lacey and Grandpa Jackson are going to bring you over when it's time."

Lucas munched on his toast. "Are you going to watch me?"

Lily helped herself to some coffee and sat down next to him. "I sure am. And Mr. Montgomery is going to be there, too."

Lucas clapped his hands. "I like Mr. Montgummy!"

She ruffled his hair and replied sincerely, "I do, too."

Her parents exchanged speculative looks. Realizing she'd said too much, Lily flushed. She doubted they had any idea how deeply involved she had become with Gannon during the past week or so, but had they known, she was sure her parents wouldn't have approved. Especially given the heartache her previous reckless behavior had provided...

Her expression pleasant yet concerned, Lacey set the platter of eggs and bacon on the table. "Any word from Mr. No-Show?"

Lily shook her head and continued talking in a code her son would not understand. "The QB never even texted to apologize for standing us up last night."

Her dad frowned. "I'm not surprised. Given how little regard he seems to have for other people's feelings."

Lily couldn't argue that.

Sensing tension, Lucas offered Lily a bite of his already cut-up pancakes. "Want some, Mommy?"

"Thank you, honey." She made a great show of savoring the sticky bite.

Lucas grinned, ever the little peacemaker.

"When does Gannon have to go back to Fort Worth?" her mom asked.

She added salt and pepper to her eggs. "He has to be in the office on Monday." Which probably meant he would be leaving Laramie by Sunday evening, at the very latest.

Lily sighed. She had known this would be the case all along but still found it utterly depressing.

Lucas tapped her on the arm. "Present, Mommy?"

Lily looked at him. "Honey, it's not your birthday."

Lucas giggled. "No, Mommy. For you!" He climbed down from his chair, dashed into the formal dining room and returned with a wrapped gift. "I made it."

"Well, then, I can't wait to see." With his help, Lily tore the paper off. Inside was an insulated travel mug with four festival photo-booth pictures of Gannon and Lucas clowning around, enclosed beneath the plastic outer cover. Looking at it, seeing how happy the two of them were, how right they seemed together—almost like father and son—Lily's heart filled with joy. "It's beautiful."

Lucas tugged on her arm and peered into her face. "Mommy, are you crying?"

"Happy tears," Lily explained. The kind that always welled up when she received a sentimental gift. And a few sad ones, too, at the reminder that soon Gannon would be leaving not just her but her son to go back to Fort Worth.

"So what's going on between you and the mayor?" Clint asked.

Gannon checked the cinches on all the ponies they had lined up for rides. All were as they should be. He slanted his old friend a casual look. "We're friends."

Clint smirked. "Uh-huh."

Gannon tipped up the brim of his hat. "We are."

"Rumor has it a whole lot more."

Rumor was right. Up to now, Gannon thought he'd had everything figured out. He knew what he wanted out of life. Knew what he didn't want, too—which was to move back to the rural Texas county and the ranch where he'd grown up.

But Lily and her son had changed all that.

They made the idea of leaving in thirty-six hours almost unbearable. Which was foolish, he knew. Especially given how independent in nature both of them were.

"Uh-oh," Clint said. He jerked his head to their left. Gannon turned in the direction of Clint's gaze and saw the world's biggest scumbag marching toward them, full entourage, including dozens of reporters and photographers, in tow. Instead of the brilliant Gladiator blue apparel he had been wearing, he had on a form-fitting purple T-shirt. Before Gannon could mull over the significance—or non-significance—of that, Bode Daniels flashed his trademark grin. "Is this where the pony rides are happening?"

Gannon curtailed the urge to deck the deadbeat dad. He nodded brusquely.

"I'd like to be here to help Lucas ride," Bode said, heavy on the paternal pride.

"Sorry. Ex-rodeo cowboys only," Clint put in, being the hard-ass Gannon could not afford to be at this moment. Not without making things a whole lot worse for Lily anyway. "You're free to watch the professionals at work, though," Clint continued with a provoking grin.

Bode stared back, the only hint of the QB's temper a slight tic on one side of his lower jaw. Fortunately—or unfortunately—depending on how you chose to look at it, Lily's parents chose that moment to walk up with Lucas between them. They seemed in a hurry.

"Gannon, can you watch Lucas until Lily can get over here?" Lacey asked. "We're needed for an emergency at the hospital."

"No problem." Gannon held out his hand.

Lucas started to take it.

"Actually, as his father, I think I should do the honors," Bode said, stepping between them.

Lacey and Jackson McCabe looked at Bode as if he were chewing gum that had suddenly become glued to the bottom of their shoes.

The older woman turned back to Gannon. "As one of our daughter's legal representatives, you'll see that everything is as it should be?" she clarified tersely.

Understanding what she meant, which was that Lily's mom did not trust Bode in the slightest—especially with their beloved grandson—Gannon nodded.

Lily's cousin, Sheriff's Deputy Kyle McCabe, suddenly appeared. In uniform, he cut an imposing figure. "Not to worry," Kyle said to one and all. "I'll watch over them."

Doctors Jackson and Lacey McCabe nodded in relief and rushed off.

"Hey there, fella." Bode lifted Lucas in his arms and cradled him against his chest while the photographers began taking photos of the "precious" moment. "Ready for your horsey ride?"

No *I'm sorry I stood you up last night*, Gannon thought, irritated by the lack of consideration for both Lily and Lucas. The only saving grace in the situation was the fact that the little boy had either forgotten or was so confused by all the changes recently that he couldn't comprehend all that was going on.

"Hey, Bode! Can we get a photo of you and your son and one of the ponies?" a photographer shouted.

Before anyone could say yes or no to the request, a throng of reporters rushed toward them, all jockeying for position.

"Bode!" The reporter in the lead, a pretty blonde with a microphone, shouted, "Is it true? Was a deal just worked out to trade you to the Baltimore Hawks—for even more money than you've been making at the Dallas Gladiators?"

Bode flashed a grin worthy of the Lone Star State. "What can I say?" he answered, seemingly oblivious to the fact that the son he held was beginning to look frightened by the aggressiveness of the journalists pressing in. "When the Hawks see talent, they value it!"

Without warning, Viviana and her entourage appeared. The crowd parted for what everyone knew would be the money shot of the day.

Suddenly, the supermodel was standing next to Bode. Their little girls were handed off by their nannies. Bode had two children in his arms, a three-year-old girl and a four-year-old son. Viviana held their year-old daughter. The flashbulbs went off. The reporters pressed closer, all of them shouting to be heard.

Without warning, all three small children had suffered enough and began to cry. The nannies quickly appeared. The two little girls were spirited off, still crying. Bode, not sure what to do, handed Lucas off to Gannon.

"They're too *loud*! I'm scared!" Lucas sobbed to Gannon, winding both his arms tightly around Gannon's neck.

Still holding Lucas close, Gannon moved away from the departing crowd and into the stable. "I know, sport," he soothed, patting the tyke on the back. "In your place, I'd be a little rattled, too. Those people were way too loud and way too pushy."

Lucas sniffed. "Yeah," he said.

Their glances locked. For the first time, Gannon learned what it was really like to comfort a child. He liked the feeling of being someone Lucas could depend on, almost as much as he adored the little boy in his arms. And he did adore Lucas, every bit as much as he adored Lucas's mommy.

The air around them grew quieter.

Gannon looked around, then walked back out into the ring, where the ponies were still tethered. Not only had the reporters followed Bode, but a good deal of the fairgoers had raced after them, too. "Would you like to be the first to ride a pony?" Gannon asked, glad the melee had passed—at least for the two of them.

Lucas exhaled shakily and held on all the tighter. "Can I?"

Gannon smiled at him, glad to be able to bring a little joy and attention into the young child's life. "You sure can," he soothed.

His grip loosening slightly, Lucas studied Gannon. "Those noisy people won't come back?"

It wouldn't matter if they did. As far as Gannon was concerned, all photo ops were done for the day. "Not to worry." He pressed a kiss on the top of Lucas's head. "I've got you."

LILY WAS IN the midst of arbitrating a dispute over the cooking competition site assignments when it sounded as if all hell broke loose toward the fairground stables. By the time she reached the riding ring, she'd heard enough from excited conversations en route to glean what had happened.

However, nothing prepared her for the sight of Lucas cradled in Gannon's strong arms. In that instant, the two looked more like father and son than Lucas and his biological father ever would. Her heart swelled with emotion.

Clint McCulloch reached her first. He filled her in on all that had happened, concluding, "Your son's fine—thanks to Gannon."

Lily could see that. She patted the former rodeo cowboy on the arm. "I'm sure you helped, too."

Clint shook his head, not about to take credit where none was due. "It was all Gannon."

"Mommy!" Seeing her, Lucas broke into fresh tears. He reached for her. "The noisy people scared me!"

"I know, baby," Lily gathered him into her arms and held him close. Her eyes met Gannon's. "Thank you," she mouthed, as she continued to soothe her son with touch and words.

"Don't you know," Gannon said softly, "I wouldn't have been anywhere else." Then, oblivious to all the people watching, he leaned over and brushed a kiss across her temple.

No sooner had Lucas finished his pony ride than Lily was paged to the fairground office. "I'll keep Lucas with me until you've handled whatever that is," Gannon promised.

Lily looked at him in relief. She really had to stop letting him come to her rescue this way. Yet at this particular moment, what choice did she have? The overcrowded chili cook-off and festival was in full swing and she had a job to do. "You sure it's okay?"

He nodded. "He can help us take tickets from the other little kids, right, buddy?"

Lucas nodded, looking as important as ever.

Glad for the help, Lily discreetly squeezed Gannon's hand. "I owe you one." Actually, more than one.

He flashed a rakish grin. "I'll be sure to collect…"

Trying not to think how glorious he made her feel whenever they were together, Lily shook her head at him—just as playfully. Then texted the others to let them know she was on her way, and headed for the fairgrounds office.

Inside were members of the steering committee. "We're short a judge!" bestselling author Taylor O'Quinn-Carrigan said to quickly bring Lily up to speed.

"What are we going to do?" Miss Mim asked with librarian calm.

Good question, Lily thought, already searching for a solution.

Marybeth Simmons looked at the former mayor. "This is all your fault, Rex, for trying to bring someone as famous as Bode Daniels into our little festival."

Which wasn't exactly "little" anymore, Lily thought, looking at the impressive crowds thronging the carnival-style games and vendors on the midway.

Rex glared at everyone doling out the criticism. "Thanks to Bode we've already broken all records—for an inaugural outing—of a chili cook-off. At least in Texas!" he said.

To the point, Lily knew, they'd nearly run out of food twice and were seriously short on facilities.

"Who cares about that?" Cady, the Laramie Chamber of Commerce marketing exec, fumed. "We've got bigger problems on our hands! Starting with the fact that we revised all the contest rules to allow for an extra judge, and now Bode Daniels has gone off to Baltimore on some private jet!" She huffed out a breath. "The first round of chili judging is supposed to start in fifteen minutes—and we can't begin until we have a full panel!"

Lily put on her lawyer hat and held up a hand. "The contest rules allow for an emergency replacement of any—or even all—judges. All we need to do is appoint someone."

"Who?" Lulu Sanderson asked.

Lily turned to the red-faced Realtor who had been a thorn in her side for months now. "I say we ask our former mayor," Lily said.

Rex blinked in astonishment. "You want *me* to do it?"

The more Lily thought about it, the more she knew it was the right way to go. And not just because she was tired of being undermined at every step, tired of her and Rex being enemies. For the good of the town, they needed to spend a lot less time fighting against each other and a lot more time working together.

"You've labored hard to make this a success. And since you were responsible for bringing Bode into this, and hence, upping attendance levels dramatically, I think it's appropriate that you step in, in Bode's place, Rex."

To her relief, the quintessential good old boy looked pleased. "So unless anyone else has a better suggestion..." Lily continued affably.

No one did.

"...all in favor of the replacement, say aye."

A chorus of relieved ayes followed. The tension that had been in the room when she'd arrived suddenly faded.

Lily shook Rex's hand. "Congratulations. You and Gannon will now share the head judging duties. And now," she finished firmly, "unless anyone else has a problem, I have another really important matter to attend to."

GANNON AND LUCAS were nearly to the fairground building when Lily emerged, feeling a lot less hassled than she had when they had last seen her. As always, Gannon appeared to read her mind.

"Success?" he grinned.

She noted how content Lucas and Gannon looked together, and Lily nodded affably. Trying not to think about what it was going to be like for them when Gannon was no longer around every day, Lily told him about the change in judges. "Think you can handle that?" she asked flirtatiously before she could stop herself.

He looped an arm about her waist and brought her in for a family-style hug. "Anything to make your life easier," he murmured.

Which wasn't surprising, Lily thought, given that Gannon was the most chivalrous and good-natured man she had ever met.

Wishing they could stay like that forever, Lily knelt down to talk to her son. "Did you have fun this morning?"

Lucas nodded vigorously. "I sure did, Mommy." He beamed adoringly up at Gannon. "Mr. Montgummy and Mr. McDonalds—"

Gannon hunkered down to join them. "McCulloch," he interpreted helpfully.

Ah, yes, Clint. The former rodeo cowboy who had come to his senses and returned to Laramie County for good, just as she secretly hoped Gannon one day would.

"—let me take some of the tickets!" Lucas finished, clapping his hands in delight.

"How nice!" Lily enthused.

"And I got to wave at some of the kids taking their pony rides, too."

"Amazing."

An announcement sounded for all cook-off judges to report. The adults straightened reluctantly, their tête-à-tête at an end. Gannon high-fived Lucas and, knowing how she felt about PDAs while on the job, gave Lily a long lingering look instead of the embrace she secretly coveted. "See you later?"

Her heartbeat accelerating, Lily nodded.

"Mommy, did you know that both Mr. Montgummy and Mr. McDonalds get to ride great big horses?" Lucas stood on tiptoe and used his arms to demonstrate unimaginable height and breadth.

"Yes, I did. They both used to be rodeo cowboys when I was growing up. And Aunt Rose and Aunt Violet and I used to go to the competitions right here at the fairgrounds to see them compete."

"Compe— What's that?"

"Where you all do something and everybody tries to be the winner."

Lucas absorbed that. "Oh. Did they win?"

"Most of the time." Clint more than Gannon. But then "Clint was born on the back of the horse" was how the joke usually went. Gannon came to the party later...and to the boon of grateful clients, left sooner, too.

To Lily's relief, Lucas was so happy about being able to have such an important role in the pony rides—courtesy of Gannon and Clint—that he seemed to have completely forgotten about the morning's hullabaloo with Bode when she took him for a quick lunch with her sister Violet in the covered outdoor pavilion. From there, he went with her parents to spend yet another day and night at their house.

Which was, Lily noted on a beleaguered sigh, something her son was getting far too used to doing, too.

The rest of her day was busy but eventful.

The governor and his wife—and their phalanx of security—arrived in time for the final chili cook-off round and the awarding of the bragging rights and cash prizes for the top three entries.

"You know, Lily," the governor told her when they finished up with the awards, "I'm really impressed by all you've done here in a short amount of time." He paused solemnly. "I could use you on my leadership council."

Lily smiled to let him know she was flattered. "Thank you, Governor, but I'm pretty busy here."

"All it would require is one day a week in Austin."

And travel there and back. And more demands on my time. And more time away from my son and anyone else—like Gannon—whom I'd like to see a whole lot more of...

The governor clamped a congratulatory hand on her shoulder. "You're a talented politician, Lily. You need experience like what I'm offering to get you ready for higher office."

She should be ecstatic, Lily noted, as Gannon approached them.

But deep down she wasn't. "Just consider it and let me

know. And again, Mayor—congratulations!" The governor strode off into the crowd to join his wife.

"Wow," Gannon said, ambitious enough to understand the worth of the offer and what it could mean for her future in politics. "You must be thrilled."

Lily nodded, her emotions a mess. "If I had aspirations to hold a higher office, I would be."

He studied her, his own expression inscrutable. "You don't."

Lily threw up her hands. "To be honest, I don't even think I want to run for mayor of Laramie again."

The words were out before Lily could stop herself.

Gannon gave her a surprised look. "Seriously? I had no idea..."

This was a conversation that should not be overheard, so Lily took Gannon by the hand and slipped behind the row of cooking booths, and from there to an even more secluded spot. Her whole body weary from the hours and hours spent running all over the place, she leaned against the backside of a travel trailer.

Gannon stood beside her, one arm propped over her head. The intent way he was listening to her prompted her to continue, "Although we don't yet have term limits in Laramie County, I think one term in any elected office is all anyone needs."

Gannon chuckled and ran a hand over her cheek. "Don't let Rex Carter hear you say that," he teased.

Lily stubbornly held her ground. "As you've seen with me, new blood, new ideas is a very good thing."

Adoration gleamed in his eyes. "You are indeed a very good thing." He bent his head and found her lips.

And that was when the flashbulb went off.

Chapter Fifteen

Two hours later, while the band warmed up and Gannon went off to help Clint with another round of pre-music pony rides before shutting down that event for the day, Lily convened with three of her sisters in the fairgrounds office.

"Nice picture, sis." Rose leered at the photo that had already made it to the website for an internet tabloid that focused on professional athletes and their many travails.

The photo array included shots of Bode making the announcement that he was moving to the Baltimore Hawks, Lucas crying at all the commotion, Gannon rushing in to rescue Lucas from the ruckus—and finally, Gannon making out with Lily behind the scenes. The caption read, "QB's son cries over departing daddy, but the baby mama loses no time finding a replacement lover…"

Rose shook her head at Lily and giggled. "Making out behind the scenes," she scolded facetiously. "My goodness, Mayor. I'm shocked, I tell you. Shocked!"

Lily rolled her eyes. Leave it to Rose—the feistiest of them all—to make a joke out of it.

Poppy, an interior decorator and the only single-birth daughter among the siblings, said, "Does it matter if Gannon was one of the judges?"

"I don't think so," Rose retorted, waggling her brows at Lily. "It's not as if our sis entered any hot tamales for him to consider…"

The idealistic Violet got into the spirit and tapped her index finger playfully against her chin. "Wonder if this will up Lily's stock in the governor's estimation—or lower it?"

An unamused Lily muttered, "Stop it, you all."

Her three sisters burst into merry laughter. "Sorry," Poppy, the eldest, said finally. "Some things are too good to resist."

"Speaking of someone too good to resist…" Rose murmured as Gannon appeared just outside the glass window next to the office door.

Violet sighed wistfully and pretended to fan herself, even though they all knew after the death of her fiancé she had no interest of ever finding love again. "Oh…my…" she said, mugging.

"My guess is that this cowboy needs a moment alone with his lady." Sensitive as ever to the needs of others, Violet hopped up and headed for the door.

Rose and Poppy followed. "Do you think he's seen the photo?" Poppy asked.

"What photo?" Gannon strolled in.

Obviously not, Lily thought, taking in the happy look on his suntanned face. Handsome as ever in a red judging T-shirt, nice-fitting jeans and Stetson, he had a denim jacket slung over his shoulder, a mixture of mischief and lust in his midnight-blue eyes.

Her sisters exited on a laugh. "Good luck with that," they teased over their shoulders.

The door shut and all was silent. He sauntered closer. Lily's heart pounded like a wild thing in her chest.

He caught her by the wrist and pulled her in. Then wrapped her in a welcoming hug that felt as warm and strong as he did. "The band is about to start. If I recall, you owe me a dance."

She nodded, resting her head against his muscular chest. If only they could stay the way they had been whenever they were alone together, the two of them shutting out the rest of the world.

But that wasn't going to be possible, Lily knew.

Still stinging from the way the celebrity gossip site had depicted her, Lily extricated herself from his compelling embrace and pointed to the website photos that were already an internet sensation. "Do you really think that's wise—for us to be seen together here tonight—after this?" she asked. "I mean, for all we know, whoever took those photos of us earlier is still here."

Gannon squinted at her and shrugged. "Everyone knows we're a couple, Lily."

She had worked very hard to keep their relationship under wraps. "No, they don't."

He stepped behind her to massage the tense muscles in her back and shoulders. "Yes. They do. It doesn't matter whether they see us kissing or not, all they have to do is look at our body language. Or consider that for the past few nights, my pickup truck has been parked in your driveway, nearly to dawn."

"There are any number of reasons for that."

"Mmm-hmm. The most likely of which is that the two of us have something going on."

"I don't think everyone would jump to that conclusion."

He gave her a look that said she was being hopelessly naive yet again. "Then why," he countered drily, "have I had people coming up to me all day long asking me what's next for us?"

She swallowed. Something else she did *not* want to talk about. Throwing up her hands, she began to pace restlessly around the small utilitarian office. "Look, Gannon, I don't expect you to know what it feels like to be depicted like some cheap floozy out for QB money in the tabloid press." She aimed a thumb at her chest. "But I do…"

Expression grim, he ascertained, "We're talking about what Bode and his personal legal/public relations team did to you when you first found out you were pregnant."

Lily nodded, equal parts relieved—that he understood this

much—and distressed to find it all happening again. "Before I had the DNA tests on my side. Not to mention what happened earlier in the week, when Bode publicly intimated to the Texas sports reporters and newspapers that I was the reason Lucas had not seen much of him. And did not carry his last name." None of that had affected her as mayor of Laramie, but if the slanderous behavior continued, it would definitely have an impact on both her and her young son.

And that she could not have. No matter what she had to give up.

Taking heed of her defiant posture, Gannon remained where he was. His expression was as ticked off as she felt. "Yeah, I agree, your ex is a class-A jerk. I'm glad you're finally realizing it."

A distraught silence fell between them, and he looked at her long and hard.

"Instead of trying to make excuses for him and harboring false hopes that he'll finally be the stand-up guy Lucas deserves to have for a father."

Lily shoved her hands through her hair, aware she'd never felt so simultaneously weary and wired in her life.

And all because she did not want to fight. Not with Bode. And certainly not with Gannon.

Sighing, she reminded him, "I tried to be fair." To Bode. Her son. Herself.

Gannon disagreed. "No. You overcompromised with him, as usual."

Lily continued holding herself together with effort. Unable to bear the pitying look in his eyes, she whirled away from him. "Compromise saved the day on more than one occasion during this chili cook-off and festival."

He clamped a hand on her shoulder and turned her back to him. "I'm not denying there's a time and place for it."

"Then what are you getting at?" she shot back, beginning to get as upset with him as he was with her.

His eyes darkened. Quietly, he asked, "I want to know. In your view—what *is* next for us, Lily?"

GANNON DID NOT think this was a hard question to answer. Or at least, given all the progress they had made in their relationship during the past eight days, it should not have been.

But Lily looked as if she had just been hit by a ball and plunged into the dunking booth on the midway. Staring back at him, she shoved the hair off her face and sputtered, "You're leaving to go back to Fort Worth tomorrow." Her voice had an accusatory ring.

He stood, legs braced apart, hands on his waist. "For the week, yes. When the weekend comes up again, I'll be free to do as I please, as will you."

Sighing, she began to pace. "I don't think so."

He resisted the urge to take her in his arms and kiss some sense into her only because he didn't want hot sex being the only thing binding them together. "What do you mean?"

She whirled to face him, the silky honey-blond waves of her hair swirling about her slender shoulders. She raked her teeth across the soft plumpness of her lower lip. "Gannon, I interned at one of those top-tier firms when I was in law school. I know the hours the attorneys kept. I saw for myself, on the Sunday afternoon we dropped by your firm, how many people were there, toiling away."

He set his jaw, too. "So we work hard, so what?" That was par for the course in any top-tier firm when even the lowliest of associates were expected to bill in excess of twenty-five hundred hours a year. Just to keep their jobs!

She looked him in the eye. "So we need to be realistic here. What are the odds you're going to be able to make the two-plus hour drive to Laramie to see me and Lucas very often, if at all? Especially given the fact you're selling the Triple M Ranch to Rex's company."

"First of all, nothing's set," he reminded her, temper flaring.

"I know Rex. It will be."

"Second of all, my mother is keeping the house and the land surrounding it," he continued. "So I'll have somewhere to stay when I'm in Laramie, even if you don't want me bunking at your place." He paused, studying the sudden shift in her mood. He understood that her emotions were all over the place. His were, too.

Her new calm, matter-of-fact expression was even more unsettling than her anger.

And suddenly he realized this was no spur-of-the-moment impulse generated by a tabloid photo, but a well-thought-out decision she hadn't bothered to tell him about.

"But that's not the issue, is it?" he realized out loud, suddenly feeling as if he had been sucker punched.

Sadness and regret filled her eyes. "You're right," she said quietly. "It isn't."

He waited for the next blow. It wasn't long in coming.

"My life is here."

Frustration boiling over, he strode closer. He held her shoulders and persuaded gently, "For the next year. Then, as you've already told me—" and no one else "—because you don't plan to run for mayor again, you will be free to do exactly as you please."

She extricated herself from his light, staying grasp. Unlike him, seeming unsure they could make a long-distance relationship last even that long. "I don't want to live in the city. I don't want to raise my son there."

Now she was just making up excuses. "How do you know?" he asked, his patience fading fast. "You haven't given it a chance. Lucas seemed just fine with my place there when the two of you visited."

Lily turned her glance away. She appeared to be holding herself together with effort. That was little comfort, given what she was talking about doing—summarily destroying everything they had shared over the past eight days. He'd thought what they had been building toward was incredibly special, surely something worth fighting for, but obviously he was alone in that.

Lily drew a shaky breath. "I have family here to help out with Lucas whenever I need. Although if I'm not mayor, I won't need as much help as I have recently."

"If you come to Fort Worth, you'll have me."

"If I come to Fort Worth, you'll be at the office sixty to eighty hours every week. I'll be alone in your apartment with Lucas."

He shook his head, determined not to let her put up barriers between them once again. "Not if you make friends, get a job..."

To his disappointment, her outward confusion only grew. "Doing what?"

He shrugged. "Whatever you want that makes you happy. You can go back to being a lawyer again."

Lily looked out the only window from the second-story office. Darkness had fallen, but the fairgrounds were lit up with strands of red-and-white lights. Festival-goers thronged, crowding all the aisles, lining up at the food vendors and carnival-style games. The band could be heard warming up. But in here, it was cold, sterile and gray, with fluorescent overhead lights adding a harsh illumination to the already tense atmosphere.

"I told you," Lily continued, sounding even more upset. "I hate litigating—it's too contentious. Too focused on winning and losing, instead of what's right for everyone in a situation..."

Figuring it was time to lay all their cards on the table, he let his disappointment in her show. "Then don't be a lawyer. Don't work at all, if you don't want. Be a mom. Have more kids. Help me find a place in the suburbs of Fort Worth and turn it into a home. I'd love that." *More than you know...*

Her lips pinched tight. "That's not me, either. Don't you see that, Gannon? I don't want a job like the one I have now that takes so much of my time and sometimes makes it hard for me to see my son."

Desperately, he searched for a solution that seemed to elude her. "You want to work part-time?"

Lily rocked back on the heels of her cowgirl boots. "That's just it. I don't know. All I know is that to date I haven't been happy in any job I've had. And yet, for a lot of reasons, financial and emotional security being paramount among them, I need to continue to work to support myself and my son."

And maybe, Gannon thought, there was a reason she hadn't been as happy in her life or in her work as she had wanted and needed to be, same as him. Gently, he drew her back into his arms and smoothed the hair from her face. "Maybe you're expecting too much from your work. And not enough from the people who care about you, like me." Maybe that was why she was so intent on putting up roadblocks between them yet again. Because she was still as afraid to risk all as she had been when they started law school.

She looked at him, searching his face.

He tried all the harder to get through to her. "Take it from me, Lily. From someone who has spent the past ten years doing nothing but work, work, work. It doesn't matter how satisfying a career is, it's never going to fill up the empty spaces in your heart."

ONLY, THE SPACES in her heart weren't empty, Lily thought. They were full of Gannon, and hope and fear…and the misery that came from once again feeling as if she'd been too reckless and was on the verge of making a *huge* mistake. The kind that could destroy and devastate her—and her son—forever.

Which left her with only one solution to her predicament. Put on the brakes. Now.

She pushed away from him and moved so the green metal desk was between them, wishing she had equal cover for her ravaged heart. Feigning an inner resolve she couldn't begin to feel, she told him, "It's all happened too fast." Her voice was as raw as the tension between them. "We've only been seeing each other again for eight days, Gannon. *Eight days.*" Furiously, she blinked back the tears blurring her vision.

He studied her, his expression inscrutable. "Eight passion-and-fun-packed days."

"There's been a lot of stress, too. Just like in our law school days."

He shrugged his shoulders, then corrected softly, "Only this time, we've worked together."

Nodding in agreement, Lily swallowed around the rising lump in her throat. "You're great in a family-law-style crisis, Gannon." It was no wonder so many women wanted him to represent them.

He strode toward her, flashing his bad-boy grin. "And out of the office, too."

Lily flattened her hands on the desk and remained in place. "But what happens next—when all of that is eventually settled?"

Gannon sat down on the desk beside her and pulled her into the V of his spread legs. "You're saying you won't need me?" He dipped his head so his lips brushed her ear.

Yearning swept through her. Lily spread one hand on his chest, the other on the swell of his biceps. "I'm saying that this conflict with Bode may well be over even as we speak now that he has a QB job he obviously wants."

Gannon lifted a brow.

"So you may not need to rescue me and Lucas further," Lily pushed on. Finding her knees were trembling, she sank down in the nearby swivel chair. "And that you might lose interest in us as a consequence."

Gannon lifted her back to her feet and then onto one muscular thigh, slowly, purposefully, invading her personal space. "Why are you making this so damn difficult?" he asked gruffly.

When, in his opinion, Lily noted, it should all be easy.

Lily slipped a hand over his shoulder, ostensibly to keep him at bay, although it felt more as if she was keeping him close. Knowing it was time they were straight with each other—and themselves—she said, "Because this all feels very reckless to me." And therefore, very risky. "And that makes me want to take some time apart to sort through all my confused feelings. And figure out just what is real and what isn't." *So I don't hurt my son. Or you. Or me. Or anyone else for that matter.*

His eyes grew shuttered. He ran his thumb over her jaw. "All while being away from me."

"Don't you see?" she returned, doing her best to be reasonable in a way that he was currently not. "That's the only way we'll know if we truly can't live without each other. If we slow down and take the time apart."

His glance swept over her, the heat and tenderness in his gaze reminding her of all they had shared. All she still wanted.

"If we want to know where this is all going, we need to spend *more* time together." He kissed her temple, her cheek, her lips. "Or at least as much as we can work out, given the fact we live two hours apart."

Lily recalled how devastated she had felt when their friendship had ended abruptly before. How much she had come to count on Gannon in just eight days. Her son had become attached to him, as well. Lucas already had one father who came and went in his life, to increasingly hurtful result. How would he react to losing another?

Lily shifted, her hip bumping Gannon's rock-hard thigh. "And what happens if frequent visits don't work out?" Still nestled in the apex of his spread thighs, Lily turned so she could better see his face. "Or prove to be a dull imitation of the action-packed love affair we've had the past eight days?" What happened, she wondered, if Gannon didn't care about her as much as he thought?

"Or they do sort of work out," she said, feeling even more

panicked, "but we still can't see each other nearly enough to make each other as happy as we both need to be?"

His lips thinned. "All these are hypothetical scenarios," he told her gruffly. "None of which will come true."

If only she could be half as sure, Lily thought miserably. "How do you know that with one hundred percent certainty?" she persisted, tears pressing at the back of her eyes. "Don't forget, I know you, Gannon." *Maybe better than you know yourself.* "I know you don't like to wait—for anything."

She knew she didn't want to let him go. She was afraid to try to keep him in her life, too—at least at this level of intensity.

"No...I'm not a patient man," he admitted, "especially when it comes to you."

She blew out a breath. "See! My point exactly. I don't want to have my heart broken the way it was back in law school, when I thought you were going to give me the space and time I needed. Only to have you say, 'no, thanks,' and move on to about a gazillion other women. None of whom can apparently meet your high expectations, either!"

He smiled at the telltale note of jealousy in her voice. "And that, too, should tell you something. No one compares to you, Lily," he vowed huskily, all the affection she had ever wanted in his eyes. "And the fact that you still have no one in your life romantically gives me hope that, in your estimation, no one compares to me, either."

That was all true. But the knowledge of what she wanted—a love and a marriage that would endure—made her more cautious still. "I don't deny that sometimes...especially when we're making love...I feel as though we're meant to be together forever, too." As if there would never ever be anyone else.

She got back on her feet. Ignoring the sudden hurt in his eyes, she pushed on, "But a relationship between the two of us is going to take so much effort."

"So?" He stared her, not comprehending.

Lily gulped. "In the past you haven't been the kind of man who wants to compromise on anything important. Or surrender even part of what you hope to achieve."

So if he couldn't do this…

If he couldn't agree to give her time, what else wouldn't he be able to give her?

For them to be together, this had to change. Surely he must realize that!

His expression grew stony. "Seems to me that you're the one who's not willing to compromise," he said abruptly.

Lily blinked at him in shock. "What are you talking about?" She had just poured out her heart to him in the hope that they could come to some resolution, some way to move forward without the risk of it all blowing up in their faces. Instead, he was acting as if she were the impossible one in their relationship!

Exhaling roughly, he stood up and strode toward the door. Impatience tightened the handsome features on his face. "You've got no problem meeting anyone else—even your louse of an ex—halfway. But when it comes to me," he said, bitterness edging his tone, "you can't begin to compromise." He whirled back to face her. "Why is that, Lily?"

The hell of it was, she didn't know.

"Look, I want you—and Lucas—in my life, but I'm not going to take an arbitrary break, just so you'll have an easier time of eventually ending whatever this has been. Or waste the rest of my life pining over something that's not ever going to happen. And that apparently is us. At least in any long-lasting, meaningful way."

She rushed after him. "So this is it? You're breaking up with me—for good? No time-out. No second chances. No nothing? You don't even want to try to be friends?" she cried, the hurt she'd expected all along hitting her full force.

"No," he said brusquely, looking at her long and hard. "Because the truth is, you're right about one thing, Lily.

Given the way we both are? We never should have started this."

Gannon turned and left the office, leaving her to face yet another Valentine's Day alone.

Chapter Sixteen

Lucas had just fallen asleep Monday evening when a knock sounded on Lily's door. She went downstairs, her heart full of irrational hope. Instead of the person Lily had most yearned to see, her triplet sisters stood on the stoop. Violet brandished a bottle of wine, and Rose held a big box of scrumptious-looking chocolate-covered strawberries that would have been perfect on Valentine's Day. Not that she was celebrating...

Finally, Rose demanded, "Are you just going to stand there scowling or let us in?"

Lily looked at the entrepreneur among them. Rose was always selling or starting something. Tonight it seemed to be Lily's resurrection from heartache. The only problem was, she was not in the mood. "Shouldn't you be home baby-sitting your triplets?" she harrumphed at her ridiculously cheerful sister.

Rose waved an airy hand and waltzed on in. "Poppy's babysitting. Not that there's much to do since they're all asleep."

Violet followed. Maybe it was because she was a resident physician and an idealist at heart, she was always much more careful with Lily's feelings. "We came over to help you celebrate your good news," she announced kindly.

Lily went to find the bottle opener and three wineglasses. "Mom and Dad told you?"

"That Bode withdrew his custody suit?" Violet smiled

and took off her coat. "Yes. Not that anyone's surprised. We all knew he was only asking for a change in the custody arrangements because his career was in jeopardy."

As at home in Lily's kitchen as her own, Rose got down the dessert plates and the napkins. "Have you heard from Mr. Football?"

Lily nodded. "He called me early this afternoon."

Everything stopped. "And…?"

"Bode said that he wants to do what is best for our son." Lily did not bother to mask her relief. "And that probably means not being with Lucas until he gets settled in with his new team." She poured everyone a glass of wine.

Rose and Violet exchanged looks. "Surely he's not expecting you to fly Lucas to Baltimore to see him?" Rose helped herself to a strawberry.

Lily shook her head, aware that although she was disappointed for her son, she also agreed with her ex. "Bode told me he thought it would be best for all of us if Lucas remained in Laramie and Bode came to Texas to see him when he had time." Which would likely be rarely, just like before. Although Bode hadn't come out and said that.

Violet studied her. "What did you say to him?"

"I thanked him for calling me in person rather than leaving it to the lawyers. Although—" Lily added, sipping her wine "—a short while later, I heard the same from Liz, too."

A short silence fell.

Violet and Rose exchanged another look. "Gannon didn't call?" Violet asked in concern.

"First, he's not my attorney in the matter." Lily paused to savor a delicious chocolate-covered strawberry. And found the confection did nothing to assuage her broken heart. "He was only consulting with Liz, at her behest, for a short while."

"Uh-huh."

"Second—" Lily picked up steam as she carried her wineglass into the living area "—as both of you *very well know*, Gannon and I are not on speaking terms."

"Big mistake," Violet muttered, joining Lily on the sofa. *"Huge."*

Lily cuddled up on one end, a pillow pressed to her chest. "Says the physician who won't date…anyone?"

Violet settled opposite her. "Low blow. You know after what happened with Sterling—" she choked up "—I couldn't handle anything else."

Lily was immediately contrite. What was happening to her? It wasn't like her to lash out like this. Wasn't like her to feel so completely and utterly down and dejected. "You're right," she said, immediately sincere, her words heartfelt. "I'm sorry. I know that was brutal."

Silence fell.

Rose settled opposite both of them. "Our point is that Gannon is still here, Lily. He didn't tell you that having kids wasn't for him after all and just up and leave, the way my triplets' baby daddy did."

Violet nodded her agreement, and Rose continued firmly, "You still have a chance to make things right with Gannon."

What's the point? It would still never work out in the long haul," she declared wearily. "He's such a city guy." He had such a *big life* there.

And she was, at heart, such a small-town woman who really liked living close to her family.

"Oh, yeah?" Rose countered, triumphant at last. "If that's really the case…then why did Gannon just decide not to sell the Triple M to Rex Carter after all?"

ON WEDNESDAY EVENING, Gannon met his mother at the Emmett Briscoe Museum in Fort Worth. Harriett had come to the city to meet with the museum's founder and namesake to consider a few options of her own and wrap up some family business.

Harriett Montgomery looked at her son. "You won't be sorry."

Gannon nodded. "I know, Mom."

Harriett led him through the collection of bronze statues by another up-and-coming Texas sculptress, Jen Carson. "The Triple M is a great place to bring up kids."

Gannon paused at the door of the glass-walled teaching studio. Because it was after-hours and they had special permission, he and his mother were able to go in and look around there, too. "You're getting ahead of yourself, Mom."

"Am I?" Harriett lifted a drape and surveyed a stunning work in progress. She turned back to Gannon and, arching her brow, reminded him, "You forget, I saw you with Lily's son, Lucas. I know what a natural father you are."

A muscle ticked in his jaw. He'd sure felt the calling to be one when he was with the little boy. However, refusing to focus on what was no longer possible—if it ever had been— Gannon moved to look at the array of sculpting tools. "For all the good it does me now," he muttered.

Harriett propped her hands on her hips. "And here I thought you were never one to compromise on what you really wanted out of life."

"I'm not!"

"Then why are you here in Fort Worth instead of going to see Lily?" she asked in a reproving tone.

Gannon tensed. "We're done."

"Only if you want to be."

Wishing he could share his mother's eternal optimism, Gannon explained with abbreviated patience, "She doesn't want to be with me, Mom. Never did, never will." It had taken him a long time to accept that, but now that he had…

Harriett studied the vast array of fine clays. "That's not how it looked to me last week."

"That was an anomaly."

His mother turned toward him and, looking more skeptical than ever, asked, "So she was just another woman with baby-daddy problems, crying on your shoulder?"

Heaven help him. "No…" Gannon enunciated flatly.

"A friend?"

Gannon paced to the vast windows, overlooking the museum grounds. Night had fallen. It looked wintry and cold outside. "More than that."

His mother joined him, taking in the view of city lights. "A lover, then?"

He stared his mom down, not about to answer that.

"Then what was she?" Harriett persisted.

My everything, Gannon thought. *My moon, and sun, and stars...* And since when had he started thinking like some romantic idiot? He straightened, warning himself to get a grip. "She dumped me on Valentine's Day," he reminded her harshly.

Harriett feigned shock and dismay. "Well, then, if she's that heartless, you certainly can't get back together with her!"

He returned his mother's look with a deadpan one of his own.

His mother drew a long, enervating breath. Taking his arm, she guided him to a nearby bench and sat down. "Did I ever tell you what happened the day your father asked me to marry him?"

Gannon settled beside his mother and shook his head.

"I turned him down," she whispered, regret mingling with the heartache on her face.

This was news. He'd always thought his parents were so perfect together. "Why?"

Harriett shrugged. "He hadn't asked my father for my hand in marriage—which was still customary if not exactly required in our day. He didn't have a ring. It felt very spur of the moment. And he later admitted it was so."

"You didn't think he was serious?"

"On the contrary. I *knew* he was. I was the one with the big fears. I had dreams of running off to Paris and being an *artiste.* I wasn't sure I was cut out to be a rancher's wife, never mind help support us by teaching school."

"Did you break up?"

"For about a month."

Impossible. And yet… "What happened to get the two of you back together?" Gannon asked finally.

"It's simple." His mother reached over and squeezed his hand. "We finally realized where true happiness lay."

GANNON THOUGHT ABOUT what his mother had said the rest of the week. By the time Saturday rolled around, he knew what he had to do. So he got in his pickup truck and headed for the town where he had grown up. The place where his heart still remained.

Once there he made his way to Lily's small cozy home on Spring Street. To his dismay, he saw several cars in the driveway and her triplet sister Violet coming out of the door, Lucas in tow.

"Hey, Mr. Montgummy!" Lucas ran forward to give him a big hug.

Gannon swung the little boy up in his arms. Amazing, how much he had missed him. "Hey there, Lucas," he said around the sudden lump in his throat. "How you doin'?"

Lucas beamed. "Good." Small hands propped on Gannon's shoulders, he leaned back to look into Gannon's face. "How you doin'?"

Not so good without you and your mom.

But knowing those were grown-up problems, Gannon grinned, admitting, "It's been a long week, but I'm hoping my weekend will be better." Gently, he set Lily's son back down. "What about you?"

Lucas puffed out his chest. "I'm going on a picnic with my ants and my cousins."

Ah, yes, cousins. The rock stars of the younger set.

"As soon as we catch up with Rose and her little ones, that is," Violet said. She looked at her watch. Paused. And squinted at Gannon. "Are you supposed to be here?"

Apt question. "It's a surprise."

For some reason this amused Lily's sister no end. Still

chuckling, Violet shook her head. "Oh, it's that, all right," she said drily. "Good luck anyway."

He was going to need that and more. "Thanks."

"Lucas, say goodbye to Mr. Montgomery."

"Bye, Mr. Montgummy!" Lucas waved vigorously.

They got in the car and drove off, Violet still smiling merrily.

Wondering what Lily's sister knew that he didn't, Gannon continued on to the front door. He rang the bell. Lily opened the door, and her face fell.

"Oh, no!" she gasped.

Not exactly the reaction he was hoping for. He put up a hand. "I know I should have called..."

Her slender shoulders stiffened. She touched a hand to her upswept honey-blond curls. "It really would have been better if you had."

Staring into her beautiful turquoise eyes, he stepped closer. "But I wanted to see you."

She remained on the threshold, her tall, curvaceous body blocking entry. "You're seeing me."

Which was good in and of itself, given how much he had missed her. But there were bigger issues to tackle. And those were best done in private. "Can we go inside?" Although he was prepared to grovel now if absolutely necessary.

"I..." Lily faltered, pink color filling her delicate cheeks. Her teeth raked across her soft, bare lower lip. "You sure you don't want to do this later?"

And give her a chance to back out? No way. "Now's fine," he said decisively. "Although I would prefer it not be on the front step, where everyone driving or walking by can..."

"You're right," Lily interjected. "There's been enough gossip about me as it is."

Gannon bit down on an oath. "That's not what I meant." He followed her inside. Stopped at the big red Happy Valentine's Day banner that adorned the entire living area.

He turned back to her, aware the holiday had come and

gone seven days prior. Still struggling to understand what was going on here, he asked, "You had a party?"

"No. I'm going to have one. At least I...hope so," she finished lamely.

Gannon blinked. "When?"

"It was supposed to be tonight," she said, looking tentatively into his eyes. "*If* I could get you here." Her voice trembling in frustration, she swept her delicate hand down her body. "I was also going to be wearing something a whole lot sexier than torn jeans and the paper-thin law school T-shirt I wear to clean house in."

His gaze followed the path her hand had drawn, lingering on her long, luscious legs, her trim waist and soft, full breasts, before lifting once again to the delicate womanly beauty of her face. "You look plenty sexy to me," he rasped, itching to forget the talking and take her into his arms and make love first, last and always.

Oblivious to his thoughts, Lily pivoted and strode away from him, one hand tucked into the rear pocket of her jeans. "I was also hoping to smell like something other than orange-scented household cleaner and sweat."

Gannon admired the rear view, which was just as comely as the front.

He put his hands on her shoulders and turned her to face him. "I always did like heat and citrus." It was every bit as tempting as the freesia perfume she wore.

Lily stared up at him, scowling now. "Did you really just come here to hit on me?"

Gannon stepped past a pile of fresh rose petals heaped on her dining room table. "That was one of the reasons," he murmured, wondering what she planned to do with those.

Lily's jaw set. "What were the others?" she demanded in a way that let him know that whatever he said better be good.

Gannon let his hands slide down her arms and took both her hands in his. Her softness and warmth gave him the courage to go on. "I wanted to apologize for tossing down ultimatums last week and acting like a jerk instead of giving you the time and space you asked for."

She grinned at his apt description of his own behavior. "Thank you."

She gazed into his eyes a long moment, then sobered and drew a breath, looking as if she had her own well of regrets to draw from.

She withdrew her hands from his and moved away.

"But upon reflection, I've realized you were right about the fact that we either knew how we felt about each other," she admitted in a low, querulous voice, "or we didn't."

He swore inwardly, hoping like hell this wasn't another breakup speech coming on. Especially since her turquoise eyes had started to fill with tears. Yet again.

Lily inhaled sharply. "And the truth of the matter is, I did." She lifted her eyes to his. Stubborn. Afraid. Hopelessly magnetic. Her chin quavered even more, but she pushed on. "I just didn't want to admit it."

What the hell? Had he misjudged the situation this badly? He forced himself to hold on. Act as if everything could still be salvaged. "Why not?"

Lily swallowed, and the tears she'd been holding back spilled down her face. She let out a small heartfelt sob. "Because I was really afraid you might not love me back."

GANNON GAVE HER a quiet, assessing look. He closed the distance between them and took her in his arms. "Oh, Lily." He lowered his head and kissed her tenderly. Then deeply.

Still holding her possessively, he lifted his head. Offered a solemn smile. "I'm sorry I ever gave you reason to feel that way. Because I do love you," he said softly, "with all my heart."

Lily's heart leaped in her chest. "I love you, too, Gannon," she breathed. "And I have for a very long time. Which is why I would never agree to date you before this." She leaned into his touch, so happy to at last have the courage to confide in him. "Because it scared me to feel so deeply about someone else." And she did love him. So very much…

He swept a hand down her spine, fitting them together, and searched her face, as if he couldn't quite believe what she'd said. "And now you're not afraid?" he asked gently.

She basked in the warmth and strength of him. "Not anymore. Which is why I was going to ask you for a Valentine's Day do-over. And then propose that you and I embark on a long-distance relationship."

He dragged in a breath, cutting her off before she could go on. "Actually, Lily, I've decided you were right about me never being happy settling for half of what I wanted, especially when it came to you." His midnight-blue eyes darkened. "If I'm going to be with you, I have to be all in." He held her as if he would never let her go. "Which is why I quit my job in Fort Worth this week."

Lily blinked. "What!" She knew how hard he had worked to achieve partner.

"You—and Lucas—are here. My family ranch is here. And, as it happens, with Liz pregnant again—"

It was Lily's turn to interrupt. "Liz and Travis are having another baby?" *How great for them!*

Gannon nodded. "They need help handling all the business coming their way. So we're forming a limited partnership."

There was a big difference between being a small-town lawyer in rural Texas and a big-time attorney in Fort Worth. Lily studied him. "Oh, Gannon. I can't believe you'd do this. All your hopes and dreams—"

"Are right here in Laramie," he told her gruffly. "You and Lucas are all I want and need."

Still looking a tad worried, Lily studied him closely. "You're sure you're one hundred percent okay with this?"

Gannon rubbed a thumb across her lower lip. "Very okay. Especially since my mom and I are doing a house swap."

"A…what?"

"She's going to be the new artist-in-residence at the Emmett Briscoe Museum in Fort Worth, starting next week. So she's moving into my flat—which, with all its wide-open space and natural light, is perfect for her sculpting, by the way—and I'm moving back onto the ranch."

Lily drew a breath and looked deep into his eyes. "That is a big change."

"As you pointed out," he said sincerely, his voice dropping to a husky timbre, "I'm a guy who's either all in or all out. And I choose to be all in with you."

She wrapped her arms about his neck and rested her head on his chest. "Oh, Gannon, I want to be all in with you, too."

"Then it's settled?" He threaded his hands through her hair and pressed a kiss to her temple. "You'll be my valentine?"

The holiday had never meant more. Lily rose on tiptoe and kissed him deeply, evocatively, promising with all her heart and soul, "For now and forevermore..."

Epilogue

One year later

"Do you like this one, Mommy?" Lucas held up a cartoon valentine he had signed for a classmate.

Lily smiled at her son's kindergarten handwriting. The letters were sort of off-kilter, but they were in the right order and legible enough to read. She smiled at him proudly. "I think it's perfect."

Lucas stuffed the card into the envelope. "How many more of them do I have to do?"

She counted the names of his classmates and subtracted the number he had already finished. "Just three."

He licked the envelope. "And then I get to help you make cupcakes, too?"

As class homeroom mother, that was one of her duties. "You do."

Gannon sauntered in, looking big and handsome and as sexy as could be. Wedding ring glinting on his finger, he plucked a chocolate kiss from the bowl on the table. "Yum!"

"Daddy!" Lucas scolded. "Those are for the party!"

"I know, which is why we should sample them to make sure they're all okay," Gannon teased, peeling off the tinfoil. "One for you." He gave one to a wildly grinning Lucas. "One for Mommy." He popped that one in Lily's mouth.

"Another one for the new baby in her tummy. And last but not least, one for me…"

Lucas squinted, thinking. Looking a little like the biological dad he still rarely saw or heard from but acting like the caring, confident father he had since happily claimed as his own. "Daddy, do babies like candy?"

"When they're old enough to eat it." Gannon ruffled Lucas's hair, then bent down to kiss the top of his head. "When they're little, they mostly just have milk."

"Mommy, how long until the new baby comes?"

"Not until next September," Lily said. Within days of her and Gannon's very first wedding anniversary. "When you're in first grade," she explained.

Lucas nodded solemnly, readily accepting yet another change in his young life. "Well, when the baby gets here, I'll make him—"

"Or her," Lily added.

"—a valentine, too."

"That's a good idea," she said, praising him.

Satisfied, Lucas went back to the final card.

Gannon pointed to the briefcase of work he'd brought in with him and handed Lily a message slip with a name and number. "Another couple agreed to mediation before they head to divorce court."

Lily typed the contact information into the computer tablet that kept her organized at her new job at Cartwright, Anderson, Montgomery & McCabe. "I'll call them and put it on my calendar."

Gannon wrapped his arms around her. Hugging her tenderly, he stroked a hand through her hair. "You know, if you keep this up, settling everything out of court, you're going to put the rest of us out of business."

Lily chuckled. "You love it when things can be settled harmoniously."

"I do." His midnight-blue eyes gleamed mischievously. "And you know what I like even better?" He bussed the tip of her nose, and then her cheek. "Being in a joint law practice with you and me and Liz and Travis."

"You know what I like?" Lucas chimed in, not to be outdone. He stood on his chair—so he would be nearly on par with them—puffed out his chest, and bellowed, "I like living on a ranch, with horses and cattle!"

Not long after they had married, Gannon had bought a small herd and hired their next-door neighbor, Clint McCulloch, to care for the herd, while Lily had overseen the sale of her house and the move into his. Now, with everyone well settled in work and school and family life, all that was left was preparing a nursery.

Well, that and celebrating Valentine's Day.

Their second.

And one of many, many more to come.

* * * * *

MILLS & BOON®

Classic romances from your favourite authors!

3 in 1 GREAT VALUE

40% OFF!

The Jarrods: Temptation

MAUREEN CHILD · TESSA RADLEY · KATHIE DENOSKY

By Request

The Australian's Desire

MARION LENNOX · LILIAN DARCY

By Request

Royal and Ruthless

ROBYN DONALD · ANNIE WEST · CHRISTINA HOLLIS

By Request

Whether you love tycoon billionaires, rugged ranchers or dashing doctors, this collection has something to suit everyone this New Year. Plus, we're giving you a huge 40% off the RRP!

Hurry, order yours today at
www.millsandboon.co.uk/NYCollection

5_INSHIP2

MILLS & BOON®

Two superb collections!

40% OFF!

Would you rather spend the night with a seductive sheikh or be whisked away to a tropical Hawaiian island? Well, now you don't have to choose! Get your hands on both collections today and get 40% off the RRP!

Hurry, order yours today at
www.millsandboon.co.uk/TheOneCollection

0215_INSHIP1

MILLS & BOON®

First Time in Forever

Following the success of the Snow Crystal trilogy,
Sarah Morgan returns with the sensational
Puffin Island trilogy. Follow the life, loss and
love of Emily Armstrong in the first instalment,
as she looks for love on Puffin Island.

Pick up your copy today!

**Visit
www.millsandboon.co.uk/Firsttime**

_ST_8

MILLS & BOON®

Why not subscribe?
Never miss a title and save money too!

Here's what's available to you if you join the
exclusive **Mills & Boon Book Club** today:

✦ *Titles up to a month ahead of the shops*
✦ *Amazing discounts*
✦ *Free P&P*
✦ *Earn Bonus Book points that can be redeemed
  against other titles and gifts*
✦ *Choose from monthly or pre-paid plans*

Still want more?
Well, if you join today we'll even give you
50% OFF your first parcel!

So visit **www.millsandboon.co.uk/subs**
or call Customer Relations on **020 8288 2888**
to be a part of this exclusive Book Club!

MILLS & BOON®

Cherish™

EXPERIENCE THE ULTIMATE RUSH OF FALLING IN LOVE

A sneak peek at next month's titles...

In stores from 20th February 2015:

The Renegade Billionaire – Rebecca Winters
and **Her Perfect Proposal** – Lynne Marshall

Reunited with Her Italian Ex – Lucy Gordon
and **Mendoza's Secret Fortune** – Marie Ferrarella

In stores from 6th March 2015:

The Playboy of Rome – Jennifer Faye
and **The Baby Bonanza** – Jacqueline Diamond

Her Knight in the Outback – Nikki Logan
and **From City Girl to Rancher's Wife** – Ami Weaver

Available at WHSmith, Tesco, Asda, Eason, Amazon and Apple

Just can't wait?
Buy our books online a month before they hit the shops!
visit www.millsandboon.co.uk

These books are also available in eBook format!